The Scientist, the Spaceman, and the Stars Between Them
A.L. Davidson

The Scientist, the Spaceman, and the Stars Between Them

Copyright © 2024, Timber Ghost Press

Published by Timber Ghost Press

Printed in the United States of America

Edited by: Beverly Bernard

Cover Art and Design by: Don Noble/Rooster Republic Press

Interior Design: Timber Ghost Press

Print ISBN: 979-8-9883040-5-0

www.TimberGhostPress.com

CONTENTS

For the legendary actor Christopher Judge.
Captain Temple Davies wouldn't exist without you.

I

"I'm dreadfully bored, Temple."

Temple laughed. The sound was heavy and baritone. It reverberated out through the speakers with a charming ring. It was delightful, sultry, and warmed the scientist's body like a shot of expensive whiskey. London felt their cheeks grow hot with embarrassment. They pushed their glasses up their slender nose and turned away from the video call.

"I don't see how. That stack of papers on your desk tells me you have plenty to keep yourself occupied," Temple teased.

London watched the reflective light of the monitors clip their husband's name badge. The words engraved upon its golden surface—Captain T. Davies—glistened with the power of a galaxy in bloom. The space between them felt like light years.

"*This*," London groaned as they lifted up a file folder, "isn't what I signed up for, Temp."

"We don't really have a choice; you know that. You're safe, and you still get to do your research. That's all I can ask for," Temple replied.

"We didn't travel all this way for *this*."

"London—"

"It's so cold in here."

London exhaled. Their breath formed before their blue eyes in wispy, rolling clouds. Their mind raced, tumbled in circles without an orbit to stop their careening. The rambling words that fell from their lips were ones brought on by depression, by isolation and wear. It was indeed cold, but the chill wasn't what pressed on their mind the heaviest. The empty side of their bed, the unused coffee mugs in the kitchen, the damned video calls—those weighed a metric ton.

They turned their eyes toward the metallic room around them and took note of the visible thickness of their breath and the ambient mulberry-hued light that cascaded off of the grow lamps in the corner. A stretch of herbs sat happily beneath the powerful illumination. The mint demanded pruning, and the jimsonweed overflowed. They were too bored to put any effort into tending to them.

Their little lab—boxy and held together with rivets and welded plates—felt empty and barren. They were accustomed to it, having spent so long in Antarctica in the early days of their career, but it did not mean they enjoyed it. They would take that chilled tundra over this isolated nightmare any day. In Antarctica, they had their husband. In Antarctica, they had sunlight. In Antarctica, they had the freedom to step outside.

In the cold vacuum of space, isolated and forgotten, they had none of those things.

It was lonely.

"Did you preheat your room? I don't want you going to bed chilled; you always get a headache when you do," Temple inquired as he leaned back against his chair. A feeble attempt at getting them to come back to the conversation, come back to him.

The screen flickered. The distance between them was not vast, but it was far enough that small slivers of static would obstruct the image. It reminded them that, despite the clarity of the view, the magnitude of the speakers, and the positioning that felt so real, their husband was not in front of them. That if they reached out to touch that face, they'd feel glass instead of flesh.

"No. It's not like I can sleep," London replied quietly. They shoved their hands into the pockets of their lab coat and slid down in the chair.

The lighting that cascaded over the plants washed their platinum blonde hair in an unnatural pink-purple glow. The illumination brushed the lenses of their glasses. With their face turned away, Temple couldn't see the truth in their eyes, and it was obscured for a reason. They didn't want their husband to see the wear.

Life was wearing on them.

"Hey, look at me," Temple cooed. He crossed his arms and leaned forward on his desk in a subtle gesture to try and close the gap between them.

It still amazed them that his earth-shaking voice could be so soft, so tender. As much as they wanted to be angry, his words were a calming balm to their soul. It was hard to focus on the turmoil when that melody entered their ears.

London turned their eyes to him, "What?"

"I'll be home soon. Wait a few days and we'll get a whole weekend together—"

"Then you leave me *again*. This is so hard, Temp. Every time you're supposed to get extended leave it gets canceled. We've spent *twenty* days together this year... it's no better than if I'd stayed on Earth—"

"Don't. Don't do that, please. That line of thinking will only make this harder. I'm trying, I am. I don't have control over this."

London scoffed. "We don't have control over anything. Temple, we're slaves here."

Temple set his finger against his lips, wary of the gossip-loving ears that lingered in the background, in the radio waves, and the circuit boards beneath his arms. It was too delicate of a situation to speak of so openly. Life in their stretch of the galaxy was not an autonomous one. It moved and breathed at the behest of the Zeus Project and its benefactors. Benefactors long since dead. Their demands still held merit, and no one would live long questioning it.

An existence in the remote reaches of the galaxy demanded militant perfection, demanded precision, and unwavering loyalty to the lies. London was tired of it.

"I'm going to go to bed," London admitted defeat. "I'm sorry, Temp. I know you're busy and we can't have these calls often, I'm just... spiraling. I miss you too much, and it's making me anxious knowing you're not here. I'm afraid I'll have a panic attack if I keep this up."

"Then I really don't want you to be alone," Temple replied tenderly.

London laid their head back against the desk chair. The thump and buzz of their research outpost droned on relentlessly, so that they hardly noticed it any longer. It would be prominently felt when their head would rest properly against a perfectly positioned chair or cabinet. They sensed the vibrations surge up through the floor against their bare feet. The breathing of an outpost so full of life. Organic, mindless life. Warm circuitry and humming metal plates. It would feel desolate without the plants. It was nearing it but hadn't quite reached that level of apocalyptic agony.

The plants kept them grounded, kept them tied to their long-gone home, but they yearned for the warmth of their husband, the warmth of a world they missed more than they thought they ever could. It wasn't supposed to be like this.

"L, talk to me. This isn't the time to shut me out," Temple begged with a cool, calm tone. It was commanding but not forceful. The words were spoken out of concern and love.

"How's the crew?" London asked weakly, unable to deny him the request, unsure of what else to say.

Temple smiled sadly as he thought about his answer, "Antsy. Hitomi wanted me to tell you hello. She wants to schedule a time to talk and catch up with you soon. Matthias said he was going to make you some candied oranges before I come home next. They miss you. We all do. The team isn't the same without you."

London nodded. They stifled a yawn and shuddered in their chair.

"Do me a favor?" Temple requested.

"Sure."

"Go eat dinner. I know you haven't yet, so go eat and preheat your room. I'd like for you to transfer the call to your phone so I can talk to you, but I get it if you need some space. Just promise me you'll shoot me a message before you go to bed so I know you're okay, please?"

"Are you worried?"

"I love you. Of course, I'm worried. I hate how defeated you sound. I'll stay on the call with you 'til you fall asleep, if you'd like. I have to wait for an update on this project, so I could read to you, or simply talk."

"You're a foolish romantic, Temple Davies."

"And you love it."

London pushed themself up from their chair with a soft scoff and a smile. They slid their earbud in and switched the call to the device in their pocket. The screen dimmed and draped the room in a gaudy mulberry-soaked darkness. They wandered out of their office and turned into the main hall.

The long wall at their side was lined with floor-to-ceiling cases filled with hydroponic stations that tumbled water across the roots of various plants. It was a chaotic, living piece of art. The rolling liquid sounded like a stream, it sounded like life, and it reminded them of their small backyard in Kansas City that they missed dearly.

The chill of the floor was shocking against the soles of their feet;

their toes recoiled with each step. The high collar of the sweater over their frame caused static to grow in their shoulder-length hair, their thinning body unable to stave off the bitter temperatures.

They stopped by the next door and listened. After a moment, they locked it and peered through the small window. The dark box behind the metal plating housed a spiral staircase that allowed them access to the lower decks of the outpost. Though they were alone, they didn't like the thought of an entrance being so open. The paranoia of lone-liness, of the closest form of life being literal planets away, made every noise chaotic. Creaks and groans sounded like footsteps and screams; they swore they heard voices. It was a horror story that played on a bit too long, one whose author forgot to pen an ending.

In the cold vacuum of space, those fabricated fears were all the more prominent.

"One of our drills broke," Temple noted quietly.

"Really? How did that happen?" London asked, actually intrigued by the information.

"It hit a foreign substance at an odd angle and stopped spinning. Our scanners didn't pick up the material, so we have to investigate. It's definitely not something we had on Earth. They've had to halt work on the southern hemisphere until they can fix it. The grunts are worried that it stripped the drill. Not like that's an easy fix. We can't really pop over to a warehouse and get a replacement. That'd take a few hundred light years of time we can't afford."

"I can't say I'm overly upset about the fact it broke. They're tear-ing through those spheres too quickly. They've already collapsed a handful of possible habitats and killed too many damn people in the process. Hard to terraform a new home when we can't keep them from crumbling and eating up our troops in the process."

"I know. The one they've been working on stabilizing the last few months seems to be holding up alright, but I do worry. Elysium is a fairly hospitable place. From what Liza told me, it seems to share quite a few attributes with Earth. She seemed excited, and that's good enough for me to place my hope in it.

"If we can stabilize it, we may be in the clear to wrap this up, so long as they don't collapse it. Still, the quicker they finish this up and get us all settled, the quicker I can get off of this ship and stay home. I can't be selfish, though. The last of humanity is expecting us to find them a new planet, and our team is vital to that process. Everyone is tired, but I promise you, L, it's as beautiful as we dreamed. You're doing good work. I'll be home soon, and someday I'll walk through that door for the last time, and you'll be so sick of me you'll wish the project lasted longer."

A small smile crept over London's face as they checked on a new sprig of oregano growing in the wall. They couldn't help it. As frustrated as they were with the situation, with their employers, and the distance between themself and their husband, the gentle yet confident cadence that swelled when he spoke left their heart fluttering. His sure tone and calm words always swayed them. It was how they ended up in this situation in the first place.

"I'd like that," London whispered.

"Me too. I got your supply list turned in, by the way, and your prescriptions refilled," Temple noted.

"Thank you."

"Of course. I may not be able to be with you, but I'll be damned if I don't keep you healthy and happy while I'm away. I know I'm failing at the latter so at least stay healthy for me. Did you grab dinner yet?"

London turned into the small kitchen. The thin, rectangular space felt a bit coffin-like. Most of the rooms did. The cabinets both above and below the counters on either side left the space feeling more like a morgue than a kitchen. Rows and rows of compartments made to store an excess of things one would need to survive in isolation. Everything had a place; every drawer was spotless. The contents sat with crisp lines and perfect angles. Precision ruled the outpost. There was little else to do but organize. The blinding, spotless white of the walls and floors didn't help the sterility of the situation.

They opened up a cabinet and pulled a drawer free from one of the many cooling boxes. They grabbed a container of salad and pried the plastic lid off.

"I got a salad. I'm not overly hungry, but I do need to eat something for my evening meds," London explained.

"Good, thank you. Go turn on your heater. You know it takes a while for that thing to warm the room up," Temple requested.

"It'll be fine. I sleep better in the cold, and it dries my lungs out too much."

London hoisted themself up onto the counter and grabbed a fork from the cabinet beneath them. They dug into the bland dish and looked out the small window at the far end of the kitchen. It was tiny, reminiscent of an airplane, and the view wasn't anything to marvel at. Not anymore. They had seen the same stretch of stars for so long that it no longer enthralled them.

Mere bubbles of gas that stood as a hellish reminder of the space between them and their lover. Sparkling footnotes along the map of the galaxy that separated them. Emptiness given beauty by the wanderlust of humanity. It was a bleak view for a bleak existence, no matter how many poetic words they lent it.

Still, the small windows allowed them a brief glimpse of reality. Affirmations that a universe did in fact exist outside of their metal structure. The research outpost, tacked onto a slowly rotating hunk of something-or-other, left their world spinning both metaphorically and physically. Those openings and their view of the stars allowed them a connection to something that once seemed so grand.

How cruel was the universe they once loved so dearly to strip them of their life, of their ability to be beside their husband. How cruel and vast it was.

London could hear the chatter of Temple's small crew in the background of the call. The conversation was hushed. They wondered what the universe looked like outside of their windows, what the possible planet they worked and lived on felt and sounded and smelled like. Their husband gave an order to someone, asked for a document to be filed so he wouldn't lose track of the project.

"You should see your *Orchidaceae*," London mumbled.

"Is it okay?" Temple inquired sleepily.

"It's beautiful. It looks like it will have purple markings, almost a jam color. The roots are stunning."

"I can't wait to see it. I can't wait to see you."

"I hate this, Temp. I don't think I can do this anymore."

"Then you should check the front door."

London, eyes watering, blinked a few times. The call disconnected; the familiar beep echoed in their headphones. They pulled their phone from their lab coat pocket and looked at the screen. The time read 3:27. It was early. Or late. It was hard to tell inside of their metal box, in a daze of insomnia brought on by a lack of sunlight and schedule.

It also didn't really matter. It was another fabrication of normalcy brought on by their employers to keep morale up. No one really knew what day it was. Not anymore.

They slid off the counter and set their salad to the side. With confusion in their mind, they hastily walked out of the kitchen and made for the front of the outpost. They bypassed the bathroom and their bedroom, the tiny spaces that made up their whole world, and stopped by the entrance. Their eyes turned to the control panel beside the door. It was red; a decontamination session was being run in the chamber.

London bit their lip in anticipation. Their hands were fidgety. They heard the bay beneath them rumble as a deep-cleanse protocol engaged under their feet. It was not unusual. Last-minute packages would arrive in the deck below at random intervals, usually with a call from some higher up after a tragedy. No one entered through the top level. The fact that someone was inside the decontamination chamber told them this was a different situation. In a few moments, the front door would hopefully open. Only one person in the universe had that security code, and they were elated.

The panel hissed and slid open in front of them. In the middle of the hazy shower room, stark naked with a look of relief on his chiseled features, stood Captain Temple Davies. Dripping wet from a fresh decontamination wash, his muscular body was slick with green-tinged water. He smiled, the scruff on his face shifting as a heavy grin overtook his lips. His usually closely cropped hair, peppered grey on the sides, was in need of a trim. His rich umber-hued skin was slick with moisture. The researcher's frame was sturdy, strengthened from the manual labor and harsh conditions he endured in the name of science and exploration, and it moved with an eager excitement to hold his lover close.

"Hi," London said with a gasp.

"I missed you," Temple said with a quiet tone.

He approached, stooped down to caress London's face, and kissed them tenderly. London stretched their body up atop their toes and leaned into the gesture. His large hands held their waist firmly. They could feel his strong hold tighten with excitement against them.

"You're home early!" London cried as they wrapped their arms around his neck.

Their clothes and lab coat became damp as they desperately held onto his form. A soft, pained sob escaped their throat.

"That broken drill delayed things. The whole operation got shut down until it's solved and, honestly, none of us are too upset about it. We all got sent home for a week of leave. Figured I'd surprise you," Temple replied.

"That's... why you wanted the heater on. I'm so sorry."

"It's okay, L," Temple whispered as he stroked their cheek, "We'll warm up here soon."

London smiled sheepishly, their pale cheeks flushed with embarrassment and excitement as tears rolled down them. They loved their gentle giant. His frame was enormous, towering and strong, and they loved how securely he held them. His angular features and coy smile melted their frigid heart. He was handsome and youthful, even in his late forties, and captivated them with ease on a level he could never fathom.

It was inevitable with him arriving stripped down, with such lengths of time between their embraces, that they both would easily succumb to their most primal of instincts. They always ended up in bed, tangled in the throes of passion, unable to formulate sentences long enough to properly converse. It warmed them, it reconnected them, it made them feel human. It consumed them quickly. As if the act of sex would compensate for the distance and time.

Some days it did. It was hard to push down those urges, those habits, and the release of the frustrations, but it left London queasy knowing that the time spent acting as animals in heat cost them valuable moments. He always left too damn soon, and it scared them. Their time together kept decreasing, and they didn't know how to express the desire for more. A week was a hefty promise they did not believe he could keep, and they didn't want to lose that time.

Still, being in his arms, feeling the warmth of his body against their own, nothing in the universe could compare to that feeling. It was the sweet sensation of life, something they needed to keep going, and they craved it.

He was freshly tilled soil, they were a wilting seed, and he would wrap them in his embrace to offer shelter from the swelter, from the elements, and let them bloom for a brief moment. Let them find roots to grow.

Temple scooped them up and pressed them to his body. Their lab coat clung to his wet frame as they cupped his face in their hands. Their fingers trembled. A relief, much needed and highly welcomed, washed over them. Temple could tell. He was glad that the drill broke. His mind was always here despite his body being out among the stars, and London's weak conversations worried him. Holding them, allowing them the connection of flesh against flesh, would help their spiraling cease. Even if it were for only a small moment, they needed an orbit to cling to.

"Which do you think'll get done first? Us or the deep-cleanse downstairs?" Temple teased as he walked toward the bedroom.

London cocked a thin eyebrow up, "That's entirely up to you, space cowboy."

Temple threw his head back and laughed. He loved that spark. Loved how quickly it reignited when they were together. He couldn't wait until he walked through that door for the last time and was able to stay. He knew that tiny flicker would explode into a nova, and he was elated for that day.

"Promise me you'll still be here in the morning," London begged.

"I'm not going anywhere," Temple assured.

He could feel their body relax, feel the gentle touch of their fingertips against his back slide down his shoulder blades. He was going to lose them to fatigue. Honestly, he was relieved. They needed sleep. Their eyelids were purple.

"Temp... I'm tired."

"Then we'll go to sleep."

"I'm sorry."

"Don't be; I can wait. I'm starving and exhausted. I've been up for thirty-one hours, so once my head hits that pillow, I'll be down for the count. I want you to sleep, too, and I'll be here when you wake."

Temple set London down on the bed and smiled. He kissed their forehead and removed their glasses from their face. With a gentle motion, he folded the frames and set them on the nightstand. The heater was turned on, and he urged his small partner to change into something warm and comfortable as he dried his flesh and found some clean clothes. No matter how many times he returned home, he would never get used to the incessant chill in the outpost. He knew it helped keep his lover safe, but he couldn't fathom how tiring it must be to feel so relentlessly cold.

"I'm going to grab something to eat. Do you need anything?" Temple asked as he pushed up the sleeves of his sweater.

"I'm scared," London whispered.

Temple stopped moving, "Of?"

"Life. *This*. This place, the lab, the... all of it. Some days I feel like I'm already dead. Some days I can't find the will to live. I feel lost, Temple. I don't know... I don't..."

"Breathe, London." Temple hushed them.

He approached and knelt down in front of them. Tenderly, he held their hands and rubbed the thin flesh over their knuckles. Their skin looked so pale. They were snow white, he swore he saw the blue of their veins roll as he stroked their skin, and it was only heightened by the dark hues of his own flesh. His large hands engulfed their thin fingers, but it did not quell their shaking. Tiny earthquakes in his palms. Devastating.

He kissed their fingers and tried to find a way to soothe them, "I'm sorry. I hate this as much as you do, and I don't know how I can help. But... I'm here. I'm staying for a while, and I promise you'll have my full attention. Tell me what you need, what I can do to ease your mind."

"A tea?" London sniffled.

"I'll get you some tea."

"And my salad?"

"I'll bring it."

"Hold me?"

"I won't let go."

London nodded. That was what they needed. His yeses, his affirmations, his promises. Without the separation of a screen to dull the impact. Now that he was here, his hands around their own, it felt real enough to believe.

"Get changed and get under the covers. I'll be right back," Temple assured.

London relented and did as he asked. They watched him leave before they slowly stood and turned on the heater. For a long while, they knelt in front of it and let it warm their hands before they eventually made their way to the closet. The bedroom was semi-spacious compared to the rest of the rooms. It had to be. The base lacked a lounge, a sitting room, a space to feel human. It was made with utility in mind, made to be a place of business and necessity. Nothing more. The bare minimum to work and stay alive.

Temple demanded more. He knew that the outpost would be the last place London would likely ever see. The only home they'd ever have. The risks that came with stepping outside were too high to take the gamble, even if humanity did manage to breathe life into a new Earth, so Temple ensured it was the nicest outpost option available. London settled for it—they didn't have a choice—but they were glad the bedroom was at least comfortable.

Several furniture pieces that had decorated their home back in Kansas City survived the journey, and it brought a familiar comfort to the cold metal space. Everything was metal; the bed frame, the bookshelves, the coffee table. They lasted the trek across the universe and were nicer than the options the rest of the populace was offered, but London missed wood and glass. A rug that once sat under their kitchen table nearly covered the entire floor. It kept the bitter floor from nipping at their toes.

It was a boring, repetitive scene. They were tired of looking at it.

As Temple returned, he leaned on the door frame and watched his partner move. Their shoulder blades, too visible against their pale flesh, shifted slowly as they pulled their damp turtleneck off of their body. He smiled. That little figure enthralled him.

"Are you okay?" London inquired, knowing full well he was staring intently.

"Are you?" Temple asked.

"No, but I'm happy you're here. I think... with some sleep, I may be a bit better tomorrow. A bit..."

"I promise I'll still be here, so don't fret. The furthest place I'll go is downstairs to make sure everything is detoxed properly. I figure I could save you the trouble, let you sleep in. You have to be tired of handling it yourself."

London slid a clean shirt over their upper body and finally addressed their husband. He held a tray in his hands. Bowls of soup, their salad, and two mugs of tea were placed atop its surface. Their nightly prescriptions awaited them in a small cup.

They hung their lab coat on the closet door and sat down on the bed. Temple approached and sat beside them. They crossed their legs and took their salad.

"Are you hungry?" London inquired looking at the spread.

"Yes, famished. I wanted you to have some of the soup, though. Warm your bones," Temple replied as he picked up his bowl.

The smell of warmed broth and freshly brewed Earl Grey filled the room. It felt like home, familiar and comforting. Like the early days of their relationship, where food was simplistic and their small quarters in Antarctica during their second tenure held little comfort. It felt like bliss, like innocence, like it was back before their lives were upended by cruel circumstances.

Temple looked at the orchid in the windowsill and smiled. "It's beautiful. I can't believe you managed to get it to grow. The pollen isn't bothering your lungs, is it?"

London's cheeks turned red, and they fumbled their response, "No. I haven't had any issues, but I am being mindful and waiting for it to bloom. Once it opens, I'll have to move it... or you might want to take it with you. Just in case. It is... a spectacular specimen. Nice. It's nice. I'm glad it survived. It's so hard knowing what will and what won't grow in these conditions."

"Upending humanity and moving us across galaxies never came with the promise of survival. We were only promised new horizons and a chance at keeping our species alive. Still, this little station is teeming with life and it's wonderful. You proved them all wrong, baby."

"I suppose my grave should be littered with flowers."

"London..."

"We both know I'll never leave this place, Temp."

London shakily picked up their tea and tossed back their pills.

Temple saw their fingers shift around the mug, saw them desperately claw at the warmth of the ceramic and their gaze drift to the orchid. That pop of rich, warm mulberry must have made their heart swell.

Color. A beautiful, beautiful color.

Something they lacked, something they missed with an ache that could not be quelled in a time of metal and asteroids.

"I was thinking about having them move the outpost to the planet we settle on. Give you a nicer view, better things to—"

"Look at?" London interrupted. "Add to my depression? A big, beautiful world full of things I can't touch or smell? Watching people run and bask in solar rays and rainfall? No... this is fine."

"I'm so sorry, L."

"We should get a divorce."

Temple coughed and tried not to choke on his tea, "Pardon?"

London smiled a bit, eyes still locked on the orchid and the window behind it. Its plain view and slowly rotating stars. It felt like death.

"Or you have permission to untether yourself to this, if that term is preferable to you," London clarified.

"What are you insinuating?" Temple demanded softly.

"This isn't living, Temple. You're handsome and kind, comforting and warm. You deserve to have a life not restricted by sheets of metal and an ailing partner. You deserve to find someone to walk with in the new world you're working so hard to build. I don't want you to be resentful or trapped," London explained quietly.

It was apparent they had been pondering the idea for a while. The usual shake and unease in their soft voice was gone. It was a confident statement.

Temple moved the tray to the side and set his hand on London's leg, "I'd rather jettison myself into space than live a life without you in it, without my name hooked to yours or your hand to hold in my own.

Yes, what we're doing is important, but they will never be the priority. At the end of the day, this isn't about them, or the world, or the Zeus Project. It's about you. You will always be the most important thing in my life. Always have, always will. I'll grow old with you in this bed, looking at those stars, and won't regret a single moment of it."

"That's foolish, Temp."

"Love is foolish, London Davies, and I'm full to bursting with it."

"No regrets?"

"My only regret is how my foolishness dragged you into this mess, what it did to you. If this outpost is to be your grave, it will also be mine. If it will be your home then it will also be mine. I'm happy if I have you, London. I have you, so I'm happy. Please, don't allow such painful thoughts to linger in that beautiful mind of yours. Please never question my loyalty or my love for you, because it will never waver."

London finally turned to look at him. They saw a glimmer in his earthen-hued eyes, a gaze full of truth and admiration beckoned their attention, and they had no choice but to trust him. In this chaotically slow, horrid life they led, trusting him was all they could do. They felt tears slide down their cheeks.

"Don't leave me," they begged.

"I would never," he assured.

All they could do was trust him.

II

As London slept, wrapped up in the arms of their husband, they felt their body finally lose the fight against insomnia and anxiety. They were fully limp, snoring soundly, and pinned beneath the weight of warmth and cotton and their husband's strong arms. The lack of comfortable sleep and a restful mind wore on them more than they realized.

Temple watched them for a long while despite his playful warnings that he would be unconscious the moment he laid down. His little lover had eaten, was breathing steadily, and finally stopped trembling. His protective nature caused his thoughts to race. A deep need to focus on them, spurred on by worry and duty, refused to let him sleep.

When London rested without issue, he forced himself to believe it was enough, believe a few hours of sleep would be fine, and closed his eyes. It was hard for him to rest comfortably due to his own anxieties, but he slept. For a while, they both rested without interruption.

Still, Temple could not be still for long. He found himself waking around 0700. The contents below his feet left him uneasy, and he wanted to handle the situation before London tried to do it themself. If his partner still slept when he returned, he'd come back and hold them. He had time. He promised them time, and he would be damned if he broke that promise this time around. Damned if he let groceries and mindless tasks steal away precious minutes by his lover's side.

Quietly, he slid out of bed and fixed the thick duvet over London's body. Grabbing a heavier sweater, he made his way to the restroom to relieve himself and, with a yawn, headed to the end of the hall toward London's office.

He told his most trusted researchers to message if anything seemed amiss or came from the research pertaining to their mining efforts on Gibraltar—one of the possible home spheres for humanity—and the unusual material that broke their drill. As he booted up the console, he logged in with his personal credentials and opened his reporting application. He hoped a quick check-in would be enough to satisfy his employers and let him rest for the day without interruption.

Updates from his team let him know everyone had safely arrived at the home vessel, *The Olympia*, without issue, but a peculiar and slightly unsettling report coming in from Elysium—the newest colony effort—stated that the research team sent a distressing radio relay a few hours prior. One backed by a symphony of screams and the sounds of destruction, and the encampment went dark shortly after 0200. A search and rescue operation was underway.

Temple felt his heart thump angrily in his chest. These occurrences were becoming more frequent than he'd like. He felt as if they had stirred up something old, something angry, with their presence.

To keep his thoughts from spiraling further, he logged out and left the office. He approached the second door and peered into the dark box. The shadows within seemed intense, even when compared to the deepest parts of space that graced his everyday life. It was overwhelming to him.

He input the security code and opened the door. The steel spiral staircase groaned beneath his weight as he wandered to the second floor. The lights snapped on with loud, aggressive pops as they were awoken by his movement. He saw his breath form in front of his eyes as he exhaled. The damn autopsy station was brutal. He didn't know how London did it. The utter silence, the incessant chill, the bodies. His lover was a hardened soul.

He saw the temporary holding fridges along the wall, the autopsy table, and the long white desk filled with scalpels and bottles. Several small plants and parasitic anomalies that London pulled from corpses lived happily in enclosures.

One arachnid that London had lovingly named Silas sat on the far end of the desk under some warming lights in a large, comfortable habitat. The white walls of the outpost always seemed unnatural with that mulberry-hued light lingering on the surfaces. A way to force growth in a space that was not meant to support it. He wondered if London felt that sensation of falsified life whenever they were bathed in those pink-purple tones.

A small wall of fungi grew in a cylindrical tube, pink and curled like coral. More small bits of life, dangerous as they were, that allowed London to feel grounded to something authentic. His own disdain for spiders left him uneasy around Silas, but his biggest concern was aimed toward the mushrooms. His partner was deathly allergic, but they refused to dispose of the fungi. He hated this floor.

Everything was perfectly straight, perfectly aligned, and spotless. Not a fingerprint to be seen. He was glad the only visible bodies in the outpost at the moment were still breathing. It was yet to be determined if any corpses were hidden in the walls.

Still, he could hear noise below, and it left him uneasy. He stopped at the base of the second-floor stairwell and gazed down into the darkness, wondering what eyes would glare back at him without his knowledge the moment he turned away. With a hefty exhale, he continued his descent. He needed to know, needed to be sure nothing was down there.

The temperature difference in the lowest level was immediately felt. It was frigid. It reminded him of the outpost back in Antarctica, of the relentless snow that once blanketed his world. In a way, he missed it. Missed the sensation of weather, of seasons.

Temple flipped on the overheads. The sterile white room left him queasy, and the walls of body coolers on each side reminded him of the excess of lost life caused by his employers, of death and decay that sat mere meters below the place his partner slept. Both sides held enough trays to house fifteen bodies each, the tall row in the center of the space contained another ten. The basement was nothing more than a mausoleum. Two more autopsy tables sat under large surgical lights on the far end, with cabinets of various necessities and equipment for London to efficiently do their job nestled into the wall near the loading bay entrance.

The most noticeable item of all was the burner. The massive cremation oven could house four cadavers; it was utilized for mass burns of problematic corpses. Luckily, it had only been used a handful of times in the nearly two years that they had been stationed here. It was a place of great need, great importance, but Temple disliked it. It made him feel as if he were being watched and judged as he continued on to the far end of the floor.

That's when he noticed a strange sight atop one of the autopsy tables. One of the safety cases used to perform protected processing of a corpse had been locked into place. He knew London disliked them due to the limitations they placed on their ability to embalm. It was often a point of complaint in their conversations. The protective layer was another necessity, but it was cumbersome to use. He found it curious that they had not mentioned it on their call, nor had they cleaned it up. They were too meticulous to leave a project half-finished.

As he approached, he felt a sting of queasiness hit his stomach.

"Jesus..." he groaned as he placed his hands on his hips.

He did not expect a body, especially not one missing half of its frame. It was merely a torso, an arm, and a head, and it was well beyond the point of freshness. The face was sunken, the skin was a sickly grey, and it was covered in mossy, fungal growth. He couldn't begin to fathom what it smelled like under the case, nor could he wrap his head around why it was left out in the open. It was unusual and concerning, but he couldn't stand to look at it any longer. He would need to ask London about it when the time was right.

Temple opened the loading bay door and stepped into the small detox chamber. It smelled sterile, as if the sanitizing protocol had been run recently. His eyes turned upward to the security camera. It blinked as it clicked to life and began recording when his noticeable motions registered against the blinding white room. He was glad it was quick to respond. What stood beyond the next door had caused discomfort in him the last few months.

He entered his password into the keypad and watched as the door shot open to reveal a corridor, long, pitch black without power in the overhead lights, and ominous in its presence. The lack of proper oxygen flow and heat shifted the environment around him. It was hardly ever used and not a soul would be found beyond its entrance. It was only half-built, with doors that opened out into the cold vacuum of space and empty rooms that once held so much potential within their walls.

The sprawling, multi-building outpost was meant to be so much more than just the morgue, with a medical facility and research labs aplenty. A place his own team was supposed to be stationed, but that future was quickly dissolved by his employers when they realized being mobile was more profitable.

The small outpost became a simple spot to transport corpses when a mass loss of life happened, the potential of study and community vanished like a whisper into the voids, leaving London isolated until death came knocking. Thankfully, the morgue being at full capacity was not a frequent occurrence. One or two bodies at a time was a more common regularity, and they were usually offloaded in the lab upstairs.

London would have called if the morgue needed to be used in recent weeks—it would have been an exciting shift in their mundane life—so the smell of chemicals concerned him almost as much as the fetid body did. Someone had been in this chamber recently, and London would have told him if they knew.

He'd need to up his security protocols. Ensure no one could enter without London's permission. Ensure his lover was safe. To do so, he needed to start with the groceries, with the task he initially set out to do, so he made his way back toward the staircase and turned the lights off. He swore he heard voices in the darkness, swore he could hear the fridge doors rattling. He was a man of science, of logic and sound mind, but something about the morgue put him on edge. Something about the lingering presence of death caused dark thoughts to form.

After returning to the second floor, he moved through the spacious lab and stopped by London's desk. He knocked on one of the habitats with his knuckle. Silas the arachnid poked the glass with its pointed foot in response, the motion slow and sleepy.

"Hi, Silas," he said softly.

He wasn't fond of the little cretin, but he knew London liked its skittering motions and the way it followed their finger. They liked its company, so he made an effort to remind it he wasn't a threat. A shudder ran through its spherical body as it tried to wake itself up from the sudden rapping on its home. It skittered back under the thin piece of rock he'd brought back from Gibraltar a few months prior and hid in the shadows.

Temple smiled and headed to the small workroom on the far end of the lab to tend to the groceries. He picked up one of the disposable hazmat suits and began the tedious process of ensuring his flesh was fully covered. The cargo hold was the coldest room in the outpost; he could feel the rush of the chilled air hit him like a freight train as he opened the door.

The steel crates of rations his crew had offloaded a few hours prior sat in perfect rows. For a brief moment, his heart sank. A cryogenic coffin sat near the door. He slowly approached and peered down into the small, frosted-over window. Expecting to see another decaying face, he steeled himself, but was relieved to be met with an empty container.

It was unusual to see one of the boxes left behind, especially one of such a small size. They were expensive, and London did not mention receiving a body recently. That was part of their boredom, their distress. Without work, they felt useless. Without death, they felt like a failure. They would have mentioned it, just as they would have mentioned needing to use the morgue below, just as they would have mentioned the mushroom covered corpse. He hoped they weren't omitting something problematic. It was unlike them to keep secrets.

Quickly, he popped open the trays in the wall to double check that new cadavers hadn't been delivered overnight and sighed with relief to see them all vacated. The outpost was built on the framework of the deceased. The walls were lined with places to house them, and a heft of rot had sewn itself into the rivets and welded corners.

He wasn't in the mood to have his time stolen by corpses. He prayed the long-term storage beneath him truly was empty. The mausoleum that his home rested upon left him queasy.

He knelt down beside a box that held produce. Diligently, patiently, he picked up the contents with his right hand, held them under the quick-rinse hose, and transferred them to the empty transport box with his left.

One by one, he ensured each item was thoroughly washed and free of debris, dirt, and potential irritants, making sure the gloves never touched, that the possibly contaminated right hand never made contact with the cleaned objects or the box.

Every non-porous container was set atop a grate. Powerful fans and strong UV rays shot down around the cans and boxes, forcing dust and germs to become eradicated, then vacuumed up into a container and forgotten about. It took well over an hour to ensure everything was cleaned, that the detoxed items were hastily sealed and set outside the room to lower the risk of re-contamination. Another month of rations, prescriptions, and necessities were freed of the remains and residue of the galaxy outside of the outpost.

He tossed the gloves and the hazmat suit into the bin in the corner to be burned at a later time. He was glad he'd decided to handle this. He dreaded the thought of London down in this unbearable cold, slowly ensuring that the items they needed to survive would not kill them, running the risk of hurting themself in the process. He picked up the crate of produce and began the slow ascent back to the upper level.

The outpost was quiet when he returned to the main floor. He moved into the kitchen and set the container down atop the spotless countertop. He ensured his hands were washed before he went to check on London. They were sprawled out, arm death-gripping the pillow beneath their head. Their silvery hair shimmered in the soft lamplight and their earrings were tangled in their locks. Delicately, he stroked the side of their head and kissed their cheek.

Even ten years on, multiplied by the infinite expanse of light years lived in cryo-sleep, he still loved them with the burning intensity of the sun. He was excited for them to wake, to spend time with them, but he was content watching them sleep. It had been a long while since he made them breakfast in bed, so he decided to treat his small lover to a warm meal and ensure the produce was safely stored in their chillers. As rapidly as his mind raced with questions about what sat in the shadows below, he knew they would relay the events of their time apart when they felt comfortable. He needn't push the issue. They needed sleep, warm comforts, and his arms to hold them. He would provide it all.

He picked up the dishes from the night before and carried the tray to the kitchen to begin his morning tasks.

For a moment, the bedroom was draped in silence. The heater slowly warbled, and London buried their face into the pillow, their skin prickled from the contact of Temple's hand.

A harsh cough escaped their mouth. Their eyes shot open as their throat began to swell. They attempted to inhale as their lungs became inflamed. Sharp, horrid pain rattled in their chest cavity. They couldn't breathe.

Lips parting, they tried to cry out for their husband, but the flare-up halted their speech. They palmed the nightstand for their phone, for something to warn Temple and call for his aid. They clamored out of bed, toppled to the rug, and gasped. Drool speckled with blood trickled out of their mouth. A rash broke out across their neck; the strained tendons grew blistered and reddened.

Their hands found a hardbound book that sat crooked on the shelf beneath their nightstand. With a weak motion, they tossed the novel out into the hall and continued to try and crawl forward toward the corridor with shaking arms.

Temple tensed from the sound. He set the apple in his hand down atop the counter, then hurried out into the hallway. He saw the book, its bent pages, and the awkward angle it lay at.

"London!"

He scrambled into the bedroom. London was on all fours, trembling, gasping with tears in their eyes. They looked up at their husband, they tried to say his name—say anything—but the throttled oxygen rendered them unable to. Temple raced to their side, scooped them up into his arms, and moved to the bathroom with panic in his motions.

"Hang on, hang on," Temple begged.

He gingerly laid London's body atop a curved metal seat tucked up against the counter. With his elbow, he hit a button on the wall. A panel opened and a respiratory mask dropped from its sanitation cabinet. London grasped their chest and wheezed. He ripped open the nearby drawer and found an epinephrine shot. He undressed them—afraid that the contamination was woven into a piece of fabric—and injected the pharmaceutical into their leg.

Carefully, he set his hand on their chin and pried their mouth open. An intubation tube hooked to the respiratory mask was forced down their throat. They gagged and writhed in agony at the intrusion until the plastic face covering met their flesh. Temple carefully slid small tubes up their nose and engaged the airflow.

"Slow breaths," Temple reminded with a soft tone as he pulled his own clothing off. The garments were thrown into the wash.

After sanitizing his hands, he grabbed a fresh sheet to cover London's pale, trembling frame. Their flesh was damp with sweat, hair stuck to their face from the increase of adrenaline and confusion. He brushed back their locks and bundled them with a hair tie.

London slowly opened their eyes and looked at their husband.

"I'm so sorry, I was so... so careful, I don't—"

They set their hand against his lips and shook their head. The motion made them dizzy as a migraine settled into their skull. The outpost spiraled around them, and their chest felt as if it had been set alight, but they could breathe. The rash crawled down their sternum. Damn their weakened system, damn the discomfort of the respiratory mask and the drugs needed to keep oxygen in their lungs.

"Are you breathing alright?" Temple asked as he wrapped a towel around his naked frame. He sat beside them on the bitterly cold floor and watched London shift a bit.

The chilled, uncomfortable chair kept them at a slant, elevated enough to allow airflow to properly move. Too many hours of their life had been spent with tubes down their throat, atop rigid furniture. It was tiring.

They extended their hand. Temple took it. They grabbed hold tightly to let him know they were fine, to stay close until the dosage of medication saturated the ravines and ridges of their lungs. Until the small, unseen irritant was purged from their body.

"I'm sorry," Temple apologized again.

He hated this. Hated the thought of this occurring without him nearby. That a single moment, one wrong move, one improperly cleaned item, could kill his lover. That he could be on his ship, hours or days away—never knowing which sphere he'd end up on as time progressed—from them at that moment. That he may come home one day and find them dead from a speck of dust or a bit of soil left unmanaged.

London set their hand on his face. They loved their gentle giant, so tenderhearted and worried. To them, this was normal, but it never got easier to watch his heartbreak over it. He placed his hand against theirs and held on tight, pressed their trembling fingers to his cheek so he could feel connected and grounded to the warm sense of life in their palm.

The machine above them beeped to let them know the medication cycle had ended. Temple stood, he wrapped the towel firmly around his waist as he went. He preemptively flipped open the toilet lid and moved to his lover's side. With care, he removed the tubing from their throat and helped them to their feet.

Like clockwork, they began heaving. He escorted them to the toilet so they could empty their stomach. The pain-filled groan that slipped out of their mouth echoed in the washroom. Temple draped the sheet around their body and left to get some water to help purge the taste from their mouth.

The basin was filled with blood-speckled foam and green-tinged saliva dyed from the medication. The taste was putrid, chemical-heavy, and sick.

"Are you breathing normally?" Temple asked as he returned with a glass of water.

"Yes," London croaked.

"I'm so—"

"Temp... it's fine..."

London shivered and took the glass from their husband. They sipped the water, washed the sick from their mouth, and spit into the basin. They flushed the toilet and slowly stood. Temple grabbed hold of their arm and helped them to their feet.

"I need a shower... to be safe..." London exhaled slowly, forming words felt impossible.

"I'll join you once I strip the bed. I don't want to risk missing something."

London coughed into their arm. Temple fixed his hold on their body and set his hand against their waist to supported them, to catch them if they fell. They were unsteady on their feet, so he scooped them up and held them close as he walked toward the shower. He programmed in a comfortable temperature and let the water warm.

They laid their head against his sternum and waited. Their flesh itched and burned; the room spun around them. They could feel the aggressive thump of his heart pound against their ear and cheek. He was panicking.

"I'll run a detox while we're bathing, just to be sure. I spent so long cleaning the groceries, I was *so* thorough, I don't know what it could have been. I'm so sorry," Temple apologized again.

"It may have... gotten stuck to the container. That happens sometimes," London said quietly as they buried their face in his chest. He was so warm. They felt drowsy.

The shower chimed and began dispensing water. Steam rolled off of the downpour and fogged over the panes. Temple carefully set London down and opened the door for them. They handed him the sheet and stepped inside. The heat felt nice. They were desperate to wash the sweat and anxiety from their flesh.

"That feels amazing," London groaned as they set their hand on the glass to steady their body.

"Enjoy it, but sit down please. I don't want you passing out. I'll be right back," Temple promised.

He tossed the sheet into the wash and walked into the hallway. The book used to grab his attention was scooped up and brought into the bedroom, placed carefully atop their bookshelf. A horror novel. Of course, it was a horror novel. How appropriate.

The linens were grabbed, the pillows were stripped of their cases, and the stack was bundled up in his arms to be washed.

With hastened steps, he approached the large control panel on the wall near the entrance that ran the thermostat, oxygen levels, and other necessities to keep the outpost afloat. He input a series of commands and set the system to its detox mode with a five-minute countdown timer. It aggravated him that the whole of the building would smell of chemicals and the temperature would drop drastically as the cleaning process took hold. His week of rest and relaxation was off to a rocky start.

The wash cycle was engaged, the linens and garments tumbled as the detox process began. Temple opened the shower door and looked down at his beloved.

London was on the floor, their legs pulled up to their chest, with their chin set atop their kneecaps. Their eyes were bloodshot and irritated. He stepped inside the stall, closed the door, and sat behind them. He pulled them into his embrace and wrapped his arms around their body.

"I ruined your life," Temple whispered.

"Stop that," London barked hoarsely.

Temple picked up their shampoo bar and lathered it up. He scrubbed their scalp gently and washed the oil and sweat from their roots. They sighed with relief from the motions of his strong, sure hands.

"None of this would have happened if we had stayed on Earth," Temple grumbled.

"It's not... as if we can change any of it, Temp," they reminded.

"I can regret my foolish decisions, though. I'm allowed to be upset with the choices I made and what it did to you. If that damn cryo chamber hadn't broken—"

"Don't wallow in the... what ifs."

London looked over their shoulder at him. They pecked his cheek tenderly and leaned back against his chest. They felt so heavy against him, the weakness in their limbs was apparent. Temple studied the red, irritated bumps along their skin. The bubbles that saturated their hair ran down their shoulders, washed away by the downpour of water.

Their breathing sounded strained; they weren't recovering as quickly as he'd like.

The hall lights blinked, signaling the start of a full detox of the outpost. Temple set his chin on London's shoulder and listened to the whirring of the overhead fans. He tried not to dwell on the pain he brought his partner from his eager choices.

Not once did he consider a break in the system, a mis-programmed string of code, and the shifting of a breathing apparatus would permanently damage their lungs. That they would wake after countless years of sleep in a panic, unable to breathe. Coughing up blood with a dazed look and limp motions in their limbs as they tried to free themself from the pod. That the first month of their bright new future was spent without them while they laid comatose in a sterile, quarantined room. That their first kiss after a bittersweet reunion would cause anaphylactic shock to overtake their system.

He never could have fathomed that things could go so drastically wrong.

That the smallest speck of dust could strangle the life from their body.

That the whole of the universe now posed a threat.

Their home was a sterile, cold coffin, and every second could be their last. It frightened him, and he wished he could be home. Wished this job would end so he could just be done.

"I was going to make breakfast, but I doubt you're going to be hungry," Temple pressed for information, trying to break up the awkward silence.

"No, but I definitely want risotto for lunch," London replied with a gentle smile.

"The most time consuming, labor of love dish you can think of?"

"With broccoli cheddar soup."

They both chuckled. London yawned and blinked their eyes a few times. They picked up their bar of soap and started carefully scrubbing themself down. They made a mental note to add some ointment to their chest and neck to keep the burning sensation from causing too much irritation.

Temple followed their lead and did the same. They'd be in the stall until the detox cycle ran its course, so he decided to make the most of the intimate time simply holding them and making sure his flesh was stripped clean.

"I need to shave," London mumbled as they rubbed their chin.

"Allow me. I don't want you cutting yourself with that inflammation," Temple whispered.

He picked up the can of shaving cream and lathered up their tender, thin flesh. With slow, careful motions, he ran the razor over their cheek. They exhaled slowly and laid their head back against his shoulder. Their body was giving out on them. He knew they'd be down for the count once they threw on some clothes and got back under the covers. They would need to sleep off the heft of the medication and anxiety. All he could truly do was ensure they'd be warm and comfortable, make them their requested meal, and tackle the last half of the day as it unfurled.

III

The sound of slow music, full of acoustic guitars and sultry words, echoed out through the kitchen later that evening. The silence in the outpost caused a familiar sense of paranoia to settle into the captain's mind again. Every noise was noticeable, and it wore on his mental state. It was no wonder the morgue stairwell was always locked.

Temple spent the majority of the day going over the outpost with a fine-toothed comb, plucking the ripened strawberries from their bushes near the entrance and loading the re-washed groceries into their bins. His panic turned to a militant need to clean, to tend to his lover's home as best he could.

He was amazed at the variety of plants that lined the far wall of the outpost. Strawberries and raspberries sat beside the front door. Sprawling stems of mint, oregano, and cilantro grew across from the kitchen. Toward London's office stood lavender and rosemary, sadly sealed behind a glass plate as to not cause a reaction. Even the varieties of nightshade that grew in their office seemed to thrive. For someone so in tune with death, London had a way with plants that seemed otherworldly.

The afternoon was spent making his lover their risotto, and the soup they requested was slowly simmering in the crockpot. He checked on them often, but they remained curled up under the clean duvet with its end laid gently over their nose in a sound, undisturbed state. A cool washcloth was set over their rash. He swapped it out several times to keep the irritation down. He wished he could do more.

"Temp?"

He lifted his eyes from the pot and smiled. "How are you feeling?"

"Drowsy," London replied. "I didn't get any drops, did I?"

"No, I checked your console about an hour ago and it was all clear; no incoming bodies as far as I could tell. I did get an update about the substance that broke our drill. It seems to be similar to zirconia. The vein appears thin, but we aren't sure how deep it goes. It hit a whopping 8.75 on the Mohs scale. Hitomi was losing her damn mind."

"No wonder the drill stopped working. Is it mineable?"

"Not sure yet, I don't even know what we could use it for, but a solid resource option is a solid resource option, and we've had few of those since arriving. I'm curious to see the samples once we can get some. It would make the planet possibly a challenging one to grow crops on but it's beautiful and it would be a good option if we could properly terraform it. Enough talk about work. Would you like some tea? How's your throat?"

London smiled and walked into the kitchen. They held the ends of their cardigan together and picked up a mug from their small collection. Temple turned on the hot water heater and let it warm before he pressed the button for the lovingly named 'caffeine drawer'. It popped open, revealing an organized tray of various tea varieties and small bags of coffee beans London plucked from their thriving plant in the office.

"The antihistamines are helping. My skin is the bigger problem. I haven't had a rash like that in a while; it must have been a mold or fungus. Those tend to cause breakouts," London noted with obvious exasperation in their tone.

"It's impossible to avoid cross-contamination on the agriculture vessel, so that would make sense if something accidentally carried over. Those candied oranges Matthias made are over there, by the way. He really misses you," Temple said as he pointed to the small container.

"I miss him, too. I miss the team a lot, but I'm glad everyone is doing well, and that Hitomi is excited about work again. I know she was getting frustrated at feeling like she was only pushing papers and not doing anything worthwhile, especially with how busy Liza has been on Elysium. I know those two are deeply in love, but they are the most competitive couple I've ever met. I'm sure the research you all are gathering is fascinating, even if it's out of my wheelhouse and I have no idea what any of it means."

"Fascinating, yes. Helpful? Yet to be determined."

London chuckled and grabbed a teabag, opting for a white blend to offset the darker options they usually drank. They didn't feel like drinking anything bitter.

Their mug was placed beneath the dispenser and the release of sweet scents began filling the area. A warm air lingered in the kitchen from the heat of the various devices. It felt comforting, a sensation that London hadn't experienced in a while and dearly missed. They loved Temple's cooking. They loved the smell of real food made with care and his presence in the room.

Temple noticed the smile on their face, how small and timid it was. Their eyes looked bright behind the rounded lenses of their glasses. He simply wished their breathing did not sound so strained. The shudder of their ribs was noticeable.

"Speaking of mold and fungi, what's with the disgusting half-body in the morgue?" Temple finally inquired.

"You mean Guy?" London asked, needing clarification.

"Guy?"

"I didn't care to learn his actual name, but Liza called him Guy because of the fungi. I forgot he was down there, actually."

"He seems..."

"Well beyond his expiration date?"

Temple laughed as he went back to the risotto. "And then some."

London sipped their tea and let a satisfied sigh escape their lips.

"Apparently, he was killed in some sort of terraforming accident on Elysium. Severed in half, pretty gruesome stuff. By the time he was brought back to the research ship, he had started showing signs of molding that Liza found curious. It seemed rapid, especially since he only died about four hours prior to him being retrieved. I didn't get to talk to her long, she was busy, but she told me that Elysium was quite hospitable compared to many of the other options we've blown through.

"She asked if I could let him germinate for a few weeks so she could run some samples on whatever grew on his corpse to better understand Elysium's environment. From her incessant complaints, her lab seems limited on space, and I rarely use the morgue, so I agreed. I need to remind her to have him picked up next time a drop comes in," London explained as they turned their eyes to Temple's phone. They saw an album playing on the dimmed screen.

"It's still risky, London. What if that autopsy case breaks? Or the seal doesn't hold? What if you can't detox the covering properly? What—"

"Temple, it's fine. I'm being careful, and it allows me to feel useful. I haven't been in the morgue in months, obviously, since I forgot he was down there. Let me help Liza with this. I need this," London soothed.

All Temple could do was relent and nod to let them know he understood and would drop the subject. London smiled. They hid a yawn behind their slender fingers and closed their eyes to hone in on the sound that came through the small phone speakers. Temple was glad to see them upright and cognizant. He set the spoon down and approached his partner from behind. Slowly, he wrapped his strong arms around their waist as he rocked their body to the music. His full lips found their jawline and gently kissed their flesh.

"It's our song," London said with gentle realization as they finally remembered the familiar melody.

"It is. I guess it's a classic now, isn't it? It's hard to contemplate how many countless light years have come and gone since this song was popular," Temple mused as he interlaced his fingers with theirs.

He twisted their body so they were facing each other, tenderly set his free hand on their waist and began pulling them along to the music.

"Dance with me, London Davies. Dance with me like we did on our wedding night under that full moon back in Estes, back in the beautiful mountains we loved so dearly," Temple requested, tone sultry and full of longing.

London gazed up at him with admiration in their eyes and let him lead as he was so apt to do. He did it so well, with such confidence, that they felt as if they could take on the universe with him at the helm. Though he was a scientist at heart, Temple Davies was a brilliant leader and a proud explorer that yearned for knowledge and the unknown. It did not surprise them that the Zeus Project vied so desperately for his attention, his time, and his mind. He was a force to be reckoned with. The very model of excellence in the world of space exploration.

Temple spun them gently and pulled their body back into his embrace.

A gentle laugh escaped their lips and all at once he fell in love again. It seemed as though they were calming down, relaxing, and he could feel their tension lessening with each passing word that slipped between them.

"Why is there a coffin down in the bay?" Temple asked as he pulled them close. He could feel them tense from asking the question. Something struck a nerve.

"Is it still there?" London questioned.

"Yes, should it not be?"

"I haven't had a body in a few weeks, so I haven't been downstairs, I thought they picked it up. That... worries me, I heard one of the bay doors chime on the console, so I... I..."

Panic overwhelmed their features.

"No other drops?" he asked gently in an attempt to garner more intel.

"No. I didn't get any notifications from the higher ups, and I don't go down there unless there's a body or timely items to grab, or to feed Silas, but I don't need to get into the bay to do that. I was too scared to check the cameras and I figured it was a supply drop for the lab, someone picking up the coffin... so I locked the door and ignored it."

"You should have called me, sweetheart. You know I'd be happy to check."

"You're busy..."

"Not that busy. Not if you need me. Tell me next time, please."

"I know nobody can get into the outpost proper without our codes, and it would be strange for someone to be here without a reason... so I figured I was imagining it. That I-I... I was hallucinating the sound, hoping it was you. I guess... this is an isolated space, well off the beaten path, so they would have to dock and de-board to even alert the security system so why would someone just... try to get in? They... they wouldn't... would they?"

Temple looked at them sternly. He didn't know. It was possible someone had been in the unfinished outpost, though he had not been notified of any attempts at restarting the project. It seemed to be the most likely conclusion, but he couldn't conjure a valid reason as to why someone would have been in the area without informing either of them. His curiosity about another issue, one that was more pressing in the moment, lingered too heavily for him to ignore so he could not focus on the theories for long.

He didn't need to add to their fears, not until he could look at the cameras and find valid, tangible reasons. They thrived on knowledge and the things their eyes could see and understand, so it wouldn't be a necessary issue to delve into without proper evidence and reasons. He needed to ask about the coffin.

"The only things down there were the grocery crates I brought with me and the coffin... London, what happened to the body?" he asked gently.

London pulled away from Temple and quickly grabbed their mug. They turned their back to him and nervously slapped their hand against the warm ceramic repeatedly, gnawing on their lip until it turned red and raw.

Temple set his hand on the counter and watched them with worry, "L, what happened?"

"Do you remember Doctor McCall?" London inquired, not removing their eyes from the starry expanse before them in an attempt to hide the tears growing in their eyes. It felt like the window was shrinking as their anxiety grew, as if the outpost was closing up on them.

"How could I forget? You're only alive because of her quick thinking. I owe her *everything*."

"Her... her daughter died."

The realization hit Temple with the full force of a nova. No wonder his frail lover had been so uneasy as of late, so desperate for him to be home. Between the unannounced visitors that never made their presence known, his own distance from the outpost, and this sudden development, their mind must have been reeling.

He slid his hands into the pockets of his sweatpants and let them process for a moment as they wrestled with the truth and its repercussions.

"They didn't want her to be lost. They didn't want Zeus throwing her into the Big Burn with a bunch of mutilated fodder for fertilizer or launched out into space because of... fucking protocol. They couldn't... lose her," London explained timidly.

"You handled it," Temple stated with a calm, cool voice.

"I handled it. Drafted a false report and everything so the higher ups wouldn't question why I had a body delivered, why the coffin would be sent back empty. Doctor McCall told them she found strange readings in her blood before she died and wanted a thorough autopsy to ensure something wasn't spreading among the children."

"And?"

"I could only assume. I'm guessing it was SIDs, but I don't know, so I marked it as inconclusive. She was only three months old... She was so tiny. I didn't even have an urn to place her in..."

Temple pushed himself off of the counter and walked to their side. He set his palms against their arms and gripped with reassurance and understanding, then tenderly kissed the back of their head. London's body trembled and a quiet, stifled sob became caught in their wounded throat.

"I miss him, Temple," London cried. "I miss my boy!"

Temple held them aloft as their legs threatened to buckle. The tea filled mug toppled and hit the metal flooring, spiraling like a top spun free by innocent hands. The weight of loss, of the distance and anger and isolation, drudged up memories that were light years old but still felt fresh and powerful enough to collapse cities. How they missed their child, how they missed their husband and the life they left behind due to grief and mourning.

He cupped their face and softly held their skull against his chest as their primal screams of anguish echoed throughout the outpost. No words could soothe this ache, could still the rocking of their frame or mend their broken heart. A part of them had been gutted and laid bare before them, and no matter how skilled they were in the art of stitching wounded flesh, of reconstructing the damage of death, they would never be whole again.

Their child was gunned down on a quiet, rainy Tuesday morning, and it destroyed their universe in a matter of fleeting seconds. London was unable to bear the weight. An inability to cope, to process it, rendered them a shattered version of their former self. They retreated into themself and became stone cold with regret, with worry that throttled their ability to allow themself to love again, to feel again.

Their spiraling worried Temple, enough that he whisked them away to the far reaches of the galaxy in a foolish attempt to separate them from the world that broke their heart. It did nothing to soothe their ache; it did nothing to help mend the fissures left in their soul from the death of their son. They felt like a failure, and it was not something a fresh start could mend no matter how desperately they tried.

They promised their boy they would always catch him when he fell and, in his innocence, he believed them. Remembering the last time his small hand slipped from their own as he happily ran to his preschool classroom haunted them. They let him go without the knowledge or strength to intercept the incoming fall, and the regrets they held eclipsed them.

Their Hunter was gone, plucked free of the universe on the playground where he should have been safe, and the black hole that swelled inside of them raged on even in the remoteness of space. Standing in that parking lot, watching the children come out one by one until the crowd thinned, was a lonelier isolation than this could ever be. Even standing beside the other parents fated to receive the same news that day, sharing that horrid experience in real time, it was a solitary moment that would not soon be forgotten.

And they felt it. Felt the sensation of separation as they were forced to come to terms with the fact their son did not walk out that door to greet them. Felt the fear as Temple was halfway across the world without phone signal and they were left to handle the trauma alone, just as they were left in this outpost to do very much the same.

It was all the more painful in the present. Knowing that Temple was alive and out there, that he could, and so often would, walk back through that door, and the days of solitude felt like eons because they never knew when that time would come again.

"I'm so sorry," Temple whispered, feeling the loss as heavily as they did.

London could only cry in his arms, desperate for something to cling to. Temple could only oblige and keep his grip strong. Strong enough to keep them from falling, at least for today.

The risotto burned without a hand to stir it. Temple's were occupied as he held his lover on the kitchen floor. The overload of anxiety, amplified by the pharmaceuticals in their system, caused London's legs to become unsteady. They were curled up in his embrace. Their cardigan was tear-soaked, and their head throbbed from the pressure.

Temple felt reminiscent of the day he'd received that damning phone call. When he was thousands of miles away in Greenland, panicking with desperation to find a way home after hearing of the tragedy. When the officer who pulled him over for speeding refused to believe his tears and heartache, delaying his return home over the color of his skin and the make of his car. How, at the time, he felt as if he were failing his family with the distance demanded of his employers. How he felt so similar now. He felt so helpless. It grew worse with each passing second.

This was familiar to him. London, in this moment, looked familiar to him. Their grieving had not changed. The image was burned into his mind; the ill feelings bubbled back to the surface. The visceral scene of his dearly beloved passed out on the couch, eyelids purple and swollen from crying as he returned in the early AM hours that morning so many years ago was nearly identical to the one playing out before him here in this tiny box of an outpost. He remembered it so vividly.

How he wished to hear their voice, to hold them, to ask if they were alright and the whereabouts of their son's body. He wanted to know it all, but he understood it was not what they needed at the time. For a brief few hours, before having to face the world without their son, they needed sleep.

Temple knew what London needed now, and he would do anything to provide it. He was here this time, here to hold them and listen, and he would do whatever they asked. So he did, with his arms locked firmly to support them and his eyes solely focused on their face, their breathing, and their needs. He listened and agreed to everything they said, even if it held no truth or merit.

"I want it gone," London mumbled.

"The coffin?" Temple asked gently.

"Yes."

"If it's still there when I head out next, I'll take it with me. Forget it's there. You don't need the stress."

"I want to sleep."

"Then we'll sleep. And I will be beside you when you wake."

"I don't want you to leave, Temple."

Temple kissed their forehead. "I'll find a way to stay."

Neither knew if the statement held any truth, but for a moment, they both believed it.

"I'm sorry, Temp."

"Don't apologize. You are allowed to grieve, allowed to be fearful, and I'm allowed to keep you warm and held."

"It's been *so* long..."

"London," Temple gently nudged their head up with his knuckle, a soft tap against the chin to urge their eyes upward, "In the flow of time, it has been countless years but for us, for this life that we've lead, it's only been a few. Your grief does not need a timeline. It shouldn't, and I would worry if you felt nothing when he came to mind. If you need some time to feel it, you're allowed that time, and I am more than happy to sit here as long as you need."

London nodded gently. They nuzzled their face into his chest and bundled up his shirt in their shaking hand. They didn't know if they could feel it. They worried that they might finally collapse under the weight of it all if they did.

IV

London masked up. A freshly delivered cadaver greeted them as they woke on day four of Temple's week of leave. They were surprised that it took as long as it did for a new body to arrive. They tended to show up in excess whenever the captain was around, as if the overseers of the Zeus Project wanted to instill a sense of distance between them. Drive a wedge in their relationship. Hoping to break their bond enough to cease his requests for time off. The fools would never know how vast and powerful Temple Davies' love for his partner was. It only made his yearning stronger.

They hated that they found the dead so fascinating, that the yet unseen body excited them. The variety of death the universe brought to their doorstep yielded immensely unique learning opportunities. New ways the human body could twist and decay. It was a rare, delicate chance to document the tragedies of the galaxy. It provided a heavier workload than their role in Antarctica did. They lived in that outpost merely as a precaution if the cocksure and daring souls on the research team met a nasty end. To preserve their frames for their loved ones in the bitter cold.

Their role was a necessity here. If only the messes that spilled out of the bodies did not pose such a high risk to their own. How they mourned their promised morgue with aides and proper research stations, the ability to receive the bodies immediately instead of stiff and on ice, so far away from their husband's embrace and the team they missed dearly. Poor Matthias was promised a position at their side, learning how to properly handle the dead, and they felt the emptiness that their young protégé's absence left prominently. That bright-eyed boy was, like many who joined Zeus, robbed of everything after waking from cryo-sleep.

They missed him most of all. They made a mental note to call him.

"New body?" Temple inquired from the doorway.

London looked up from the sink as they washed their hands. "Yes. I haven't looked at it yet. Would you mind helping me get it onto the table? I don't want to drop it."

"You know I don't mind. Let me suit up and I'll go get them. Any notes?"

"A miner. Died in a tunnel accident of some sort on Elysium. During one of their expeditions, the vic suddenly stopped radioing. When they pulled her back out ten minutes later she was already dead. No visible wounds."

"Anyone else on the team report any issues?"

"No," London shook their head and grabbed a hazmat suit. "They roped off the tunnel shortly after, so no one else has been that deep, at least not at of the time of delivery. That's why I wanted to get this taken care of ASAP, in case our lovely employers try to force anyone else down there before we have answers."

"Do you think it's a toxin?" Temple asked as he grabbed a hazmat suit of his own.

"Or a lack of oxygen. Just because a few of these orbs are listed as '*hospitable-positive*' doesn't mean they are. Certain pockets in the crust may not have breathable air. It can be easy to suffocate if the terraforming efforts weren't completed properly. The universe is more vast and unknowable than those idiots realize. They can never fathom how cruel these giants can be. They've incited deicide, and the old gods are angry."

Temple looked at them sternly for a moment. They were right, of course, but their poetic bluntness never ceased to surprise him. Only they would liken the desolate chunks of rocks to otherworldly entities. At times, though, that seemed to be the most appropriate descriptor for them. The uncharted orbs they claimed and collapsed seemed to fight back with an almost sentient energy. Old gods indeed, and it would not surprise him to know they were angered at humanity's hubris.

"Make sure you're cinched up tight, just in case," he requested.

"I'm doubling up my suits. I'll break out the extra autopsy table cover if I need to. It's too restricting and it slows down my work, so I'd rather not use it if I don't have to, and the doubled suits seem to help. I'll be mindful, though."

Temple slid gloves on and masked up. He ensured his eyes were covered and headed into the loading bay with the gurney in tow to grab the new body with a bit of contempt in his motions and expression. The unexpected work project in the form of a soul stripped from the universe far too soon was taking up valuable time. No, it wasn't her fault she met a grisly end, but it enraged him, nonetheless.

His short leave had gone by too quickly. Each day felt as if it were mere seconds, here and gone in the blink of an eye. London smiled and had color back in their cheeks despite the emotional ups and downs of the first day. They ate as they should and often joined Temple in the kitchen to cook meals. They were thriving again, they felt human again, and it broke his heart to know that he'd have to leave them soon. He worried they may not recover this time.

The new body in the bay had been placed inside one of the wall coolers. A small light blinked green to notify the residents of the outpost that the chiller was occupied, set at a steady 40 degrees Fahrenheit. The expensive coffin that was there a few days prior was finally retrieved, presumably offloaded when the new cadaver was brought in. He was glad he installed the security protocol in all of the exterior doors. The thought of their employers having access to the bays angered him enough. He didn't want them waltzing into the outpost freely, so knowing all of the interior doors could only be opened by himself and London helped ease his worries while he was away.

He approached the wall and hit the release button. The tray popped open, revealing a woman with tan skin and milky eyes hidden behind dust covered safety glasses. She looked young. It appeared as if she had been hastily loaded. Her ventilation gear was still present over her mouth, and her headlamp sat crooked on her forehead, blinking softly as the battery struggled against the deep freeze.

It angered him that she was not in a body bag, that the dust and soil on her skin and clothes now lingered in the air. Another detox would be required because of Zeus' negligence.

He grabbed the thin tray she was on and shifted it onto the gurney. Out of precaution, he draped a tarp over her to help keep some of the unknown debris from flying off during transport.

"London!"

"Yes?"

"Get your respiratory gear on!" Temple demanded, "The body's a mess, and there's no bag!"

"Alright, one moment! Thank you!"

Temple gave them a few minutes before he wheeled the body into the main room. London, now wearing a respirator that whirred aggressively in the quiet, approached and helped Temple transfer the miner's body onto the autopsy table. They tilted their head to the side and gazed down at her after removing the tarp and disposing of it with haste.

"Thank you. I'll be up for breakfast in a bit," London mumbled.

"Would you like help? I can take notes for you," Temple offered.

"Do you mind? It would speed things up if I didn't have to stop every ten seconds to take notes and photos."

"You know I don't mind if it means I get to spend more time with you."

Temple picked up the medical tablet and booted it up. He watched as London began carefully undressing the corpse. He found their process so curious. Every body was merely an *it* to them, faceless husks without attributes to note. Still, they handled them with care, removed their garments with delicate motions to ensure they could be returned to their loved ones with dignity. He wondered how their process differed with the McCalls' girl, how much extra time was given to that small body and how many of their strict, self-imposed rules and procedures they sacrificed for her. How cathartic it may have been for them in a morbid, twisted way.

"I'm proud of you. Back when we first met, you ran out of the morgue and threw up. I never thought I'd see the day you'd offer to assist me," London teased.

"Well, an introduction over the recently deceased body—especially the body of my research aide—with your hands deep in his chest cavity would rattle anyone," Temple chided.

"Yet you came back," London reminded.

"I couldn't help it. You spent the first three weeks of the mission holed up in your quarters and only came out once there was a body to root around in. I was curious... and I saw your lips curl beneath your mask, so I had to give you a piece of my mind for being so damn disrespectful."

"Oh, yes, the scolding I received was so brutal. I still haven't recovered."

Temple laughed and grabbed a stylus from the desk, ready to begin jotting down important information as his partner relayed it. He loved that cocky, spitfire attitude. Despite the tragedy and pain that quelled their fiery spirit over the years, that quick-witted and sharp-tongued banter remained. It was what drew him to them in the first place. He liked their lack of decorum when they were flustered and how fast they were to shoot back when they felt offended.

"That's... odd," London mused.

"What's odd? Are you alright?" Temple asked worriedly as he turned back to the body. He looked down at the cadaver's chest and noticed it was blackened, the flesh looked scorched, and her ribcage appeared sunken.

"Is that a burn?" Temple inquired.

"I don't know. Get a respirator on, please," London requested.

Temple nodded and moved to the supply cabinet. He grabbed a respirator and secured it over his surgical mask. With a quick tap, it engaged. The small fan whirred to life. He watched as London pulled the heavy breathing apparatus from the miner's face. A puff of black smoke escaped her lips like a sharp exhale of tobacco smoke.

London stepped back defensively and watched the speckled cloud linger in the air.

"London—"

"I'm moving," London assured as they stepped toward the wall.

Temple grabbed the hand-vac from its charging port. He flipped it on and sucked up the strange substance, taking extra care to seal the nozzle when he was done. Carefully, he removed the small vial attached to the rear of the device. He held it up to the light and watched the black spots dance inside of the blue-white container. It would need to be shipped off to the research team for proper analysis.

He refused to let his lover touch it, but they needed to know what it was.

He noticed his partner staring at the corpse intently.

"L?"

"This is strange. I'm not sure how to approach this," London mumbled.

"I don't want you working on this," Temple said angrily.

"I need to, Temp. We'll need to detox that body tray... Can you seal off the lab for me? I don't want this escaping. I'm going to use a case to conduct the autopsy, but I'd rather ensure we don't need to do another full outpost detox."

Temple looked at them for a moment. They were solely focused on the body, their eyes never once met his in the exchange. That was typical of them. They hated eye contact, yet they could lock eyes with a corpse without issue. That was how he knew they loved him. They would look at him with a tenderness in their gaze, focus on him without pulling away, and they refused to offer that to anyone else.

He cursed under his breath at their stubbornness and closed the door. Damn Zeus for sending these deadly cases to his lover. They had other morgues, other embalmers, but it felt as if every dangerous body ended up in his home.

He placed the contaminant-filled container in the biohazard fridge and walked to London's side. He tapped his finger against the underside of their chin with his knuckle and called them back to the present moment.

They looked up at him, "Yes?"

"Be careful," he demanded.

"Yes."

They grabbed one of the face shields that hung on the wall to add another layer of protection. They deposited the corpse's respiratory equipment into an airtight biohazard container and walked back to the table. Aggressively, they grabbed her face and pinched, forcing her mouth open. Nothing else escaped her lips, but they noticed her gums were pitch black and her tongue appeared shriveled. A few of her teeth fell down the back of her throat.

They removed the remaining garments and tossed them into the container. It was sealed, and the date was marked on the label along with the body's name, knowing full well their superiors would want its contents as evidence despite any warnings given that it would be dangerous. Carefully, they placed their scalpel and a few other tools beside the body and stepped away.

Temple placed the airtight autopsy container over the naked frame and sealed it. The clear case locked into small ridges on the table, keeping any further contaminants from escaping. London slid their hands into the thick protective gloves attached to the case. It was cumbersome, but it offered an extra layer of security in uncertain situations such as this.

They picked up their trusty scalpel and pierced her blackened skin. The prominent veins beneath her flesh concerned them. They looked too thick, almost unnatural. As the blade slid over her sternum, the skin pulled away like taut leather released from a heavy stretch. It peeled too easily. The layers of muscle and sinew they expected to find, expected to offer resistance, were not present. Nor was the blood.

The chest cavity was empty, scorched, and dusty. The ribcage shattered in several places after the cut was made, sending greyed bones tumbling downward. The organs within crumbled and fell into the husk, as if the severing of her flesh caused her structure to finally collapse. The body practically deflated.

Something slithered beneath the mounds of ash and now-limp skin, wriggling and frantic. Long, writhing forms moved with frightening speed away from the newly formed hole. Those thick, shocking veins were not veins. Something still lived inside of the corpse.

"We need to let the higher-ups know, now. This is bad," London said aggressively.

Temple set the medical tablet atop the clear case and hit record, letting the device capture the strange scene in crystal-clear quality. Irrefutable proof would be needed to convince their employers that forward movement on this project needed to cease. This possible planet was not worth terraforming, not with risks as terrifying as this hiding beneath the surface. Damn it all to hell, they just couldn't make it work.

"Where... did this body come from?" Temple inquired.

"Elysium," London replied lowly.

"Are you going to burn her?" he asked.

"I... don't know. We can't very well put it in long-term storage downstairs. If they're still moving after being in a chiller tray for as long as they were I doubt the body boxes will help. It needs to be cremated, but I don't know how we could get it off the table without opening ourselves up to those... things," they said with a queasy tone.

The corpse jerked as a rush of the unidentified parasites flooded her left leg. The toes wiggled, and the foot bounced. Temple groaned out in disgust. The quick scattering made London pause. They turned their eyes up to the bright light above.

"I wonder if... the light irritate them," they mused. "Perhaps they crawled in through her ear or... other orifices while she was in the cave after getting disturbed by the destruction."

Temple moved to the desk and riffled through the drawers. The emergency flashlight hit the side of the metal container from the force at which he snapped it open. He grabbed the device and positioned himself by the head of the victim. The high-powered beam flickered on.

The miner's leg began to swell as the alien creatures fled. The skin stretched and cracked. He turned to London as he lowered the flashlight to keep the limb from bursting.

"What do we do?" London asked, voice cracking with worry.

"Give me a second to think this through. We need to burn it," he replied.

"Obviously, but transporting the body to the oven is a risk. We have to get it out of the protective case, and I'm not sure I like the odds of us being able to get out of this without becoming infected ourselves or having them escape. The last thing we need is an infestation."

Temple looked at the body. The unnatural jerking of the rigor mortis infected frame. One of the long, slender black anomalies wriggled out of the corpse's nose and quickly retreated once its head met the harsh lights above.

"We'll need to run the detox twice, wipe down the tray, offload the biohazard bin into the exterior holding bay. Oh, God... we... we—"

"London, don't accelerate your breathing. Don't irritate your lungs. Step away. The biggest priority right now is *you*. Don't compromise yourself. Power on the oven while I transfer these notes from the tablet to your office, then toss your hazmat suit into the burner and go shower but keep your respirator on until you're in the stall. Run your detox setting, twice. I'll handle clean up down here while—"

"Are you insane? You can't handle this on your own! What if something happens?" London shrieked.

"London... breathe. I need you to go get my spacesuit. It's hanging in the decontamination chamber upstairs. It's airtight, and I'll have an enclosed space to handle any stragglers that may get away. They do seem to be sensitive to the light, so I'm going to ensure I'm not casting any shadows over the cut you made and do this as carefully as possible.

Maybe you should make a bigger hole to help deter any runaways, but I don't think that will be an issue. It'll be alright. *You* need to get to safety and let the higher-ups know before more people die, before this starts spreading to the rest of that mining team."

London pondered the proposition. They turned their eyes slowly to the corpse and ran the scenarios, every possible outcome. With a heavy sigh, they slid their arms back into the gloves and drove the scalpel further down her abdomen until she was flayed open from sternum to naval. The body's limbs swelled as the nest was disturbed. The writhing occupants fled for the safety of digits and knuckles. The skull twitched, and the fingers tapped the autopsy table with frantic speed.

The embalmer moved to the burner on the far wall and powered it on. The oven sprang to life with a loud groan, turning the panel red as the engine warmed itself for the heft of output that would be required of it shortly.

"I'll be right back," they promised.

"I know," he replied with a calm, gentle tone.

London retreated to their office, hair dripping wet with their thumbnail between their teeth as they gnawed nervously on it. They sat with their legs pulled up to their chest, listening for movement below. A small device at their side made aggressive noises as it processed their panels. Tiny vials of their plasma spun in circles, and the phlebotomy tubing still hung from their arm, dripping blood down onto the floor.

The last few minutes were a blur of panicked, anxious movements and racing thoughts. They were well aware that a mere few moments could feel like an eternity under duress, and it felt as if the brief period of anxiety had aged them by light years. They swore new universes exploded into existence and ran an entire lifecycle in that time. It was agonizing.

"L?"

They lifted their eyes, "Are you alright?"

Temple poked his head into the office and nodded. He removed the helmet and held it under his arm. Sweat ran down his brow, and the green-tinged water from a sanitation wash dripped off of his suit. The surgical mask over his face stuck to his jaw from the perspiration.

"The body's burning. A full sanitation cycle is being run in the lab, and I dropped your scalpel and tools in the cleaner. I sprayed down the safety case and left it sitting with the opening facing up so it can catch the detox. The biohazard bin has been sealed and moved into the bay right by the loading door. I started a full bleach and UV cycle over the entire floor, that fridge tray has been sanitized, and I burned your PPE."

"And the... things?"

"None escaped. I kept the lab locked, just in case, but it looks like we're in the clear. I would suggest letting the oven burn for a long while out of precaution, and you should probably feed Silas. The little shit looked spooked from all of the noise. I almost feel bad. I'm going to go re-detox and hang my suit back up. Did you get the report sent?"

"More or less. I want to run your panels. Just to be safe."

Temple nodded firmly to let them know he understood and would do as they requested. He left and headed down the hall. London let out a heavy, anxious sigh. They didn't feel as confident in his words as they usually did. Nothing in the way he spoke would lead them to believe that he was lying, but the unknown of it all burrowed into their grey matter and planted the seeds of doubt. They would water it and nurture it, despite their best efforts to de-weed the landscape of their mind. This moment would grow into a burdensome weed they were unsure they could kill.

The situation would not leave them easily. Anticipation was a cruel mistress, one London was well acquainted with. They wished she would find someone else to bother with her incessant wiles. To keep their mind calm, they turned on the security camera for the lab and watched the footage that was obscured by the colors and motions of the sanitation cycle. They could see Silas crawl beneath the slanted rock in its habitat, bothered by the harsh lights and noises in the usually quiet space.

Temple returned with soft footsteps. He washed his body in the uncomfortably large entrance bay, ensured his gear was set aside to be cleaned, and hastily dressed himself. The look in his partner's eyes worried him, so he made a hasty return to their side. After dredging up the painful memories of Hunter and their loss, he worried that they would start to spiral with the building momentum of a possible second death they could not control.

They hadn't moved. The lost, dazed expression sent a shockwave of concern down his spine. At least they seemed to be breathing alright; no irritants had managed to slip into their system. He pulled a cotton shirt over his body and approached. Tears ran down their cheeks, amplified behind the large lenses of their glasses. Temple knelt down in front of them, carefully removed the needle from the crease in their arm, and took their hand in his own.

"You're alright," he assured.

"What if I wasn't? What would have happened if you weren't here?" they asked wearily.

He didn't know. He hated the thought as much as they did.

"I think I should request an assistant—"

"No!" London barked. "I don't need an assistant! I need you!"

"Okay, okay. I'm sorry, you're right."

They sniffled and turned away out of embarrassment. He chuckled a bit and brought their knuckles to his lips. He softly kissed their skin and waited to see what they needed. What would help ease this wear?

"I do hope you know that I am still desperately trying to get Matthias transferred. I know he's not me—I know you'd rather have me—but he misses you, and he came all this way to be your assistant. That's what I meant. I would never subject you to living with a stranger that would invade your space and your process. I should have elaborated, I'm sorry," Temple explained.

"I'm tired," they mumbled. It was the only complete thought they could conjure.

They both knew the embalmer wasn't tired. Not truly.

They were anxious and depressed, and their overwhelmed mind called out for relief in the form of sleep. The weak trembling of their frame and reddening of their eyes signified that a limit had been met, broken, and buried. What they needed was silence, a safe place to hide, and a closed door to keep the horrors at bay. To them, that meant sleep. It meant curling up in bed and finding release from the binds of anxiety. He needed to honor that.

The bloodwork machine beeped. A pop-up appeared on the computer behind them, showcasing no signs of abnormality in their system. Low iron levels were present, but it was common for them. They sighed with obvious relief.

"Go back to bed, then," he told them with understanding in his tone.

"Come with me," they stated. Not a request, but a command.

"I'd love nothing more. Let's start my panels, I'll make some tea, read you a book, and hold you tenderly for as long as you need."

London nodded. They pulled the vials of their blood out of the device and set them on the counter behind them. The plasma sloshed inside. They grabbed their phlebotomy kit and wrapped a tourniquet around their husband's arm. He sat on the floor and let them pierce his skin. He loved watching their sure, slender fingers at work. They were born to do this, born to slice and stitch up bodies.

"Do you remember the first time we had coffee?" Temple asked.

"I do. It was 0325 in the morning and that brutal Antarctic sunlight kept me awake. You knocked on my door with cups of subpar regulation coffee in your hands and invited yourself into the morgue like you owned the place," London replied sternly.

"It was my project," he reminded.

London cut their eyes to him, "And it was *my* morgue. Why do you ask?"

"Do you remember what I told you that day?"

London pursed their lips for a moment as they slid a vial into the tubing. Blood rapidly rolled down the clear tube.

"Not particularly. You said a lot that day, so I lost most of the words a long time ago. You've always been a bit of a chatterbox. I remember you tried to smooth talk me and that I was rude and irritable due to the stress but, if I'm honest, I don't recall the specifics," they admitted.

"I told you you had beautiful hands, that watching you work was like watching a painter craft a masterpiece. The first thing I noticed when I walked into that morgue was how sure your hands were. How you kept working while you locked eyes with me and never once let your fingers slip."

"That does sound familiar. Why bring it up?"

"Your hands are strong, London. You've been working so hard, but not once have you let what's happened to you cause a misplaced nick or too long slice. You are so professional, even in the midst of this hell, and I'm still entranced by the motions of your fingers. I can tell they're tired; you're allowed to be tired. And I love you. That's all."

London switched out the vials and smiled a bit. Their cheeks were still damp from the tears, but they felt a calming sense wash over them as they sat in the darkness with their lover at their side, soaked with a layer of a harsh pink-purple from the grow lights in the corner. They could smell the mint in the hall as the ventilation unit kicked in, picking up the pungent smell with its forceful motions. They wanted to capture this feeling, this safety, and bottle it up.

Temple wiped the tears away and gently held their face.

"Can I have some wine?" London whispered.

"Of course. I'll go turn on the heater, too. It's going to be alright, L."

London nodded. They grabbed a cotton ball and placed it against the needle before they removed it from Temple's arm. They adhered a bandage to help staunch the bleeding. He stood, kissed their cheek, and let them finish setting up the device to ensure his health was optimal.

Temple wandered into the bedroom and turned on the heater. He placed his hands on his hips and exhaled out angrily. The stress of the previous half hour finally hit him. The weird and wonderful universe he uprooted them to had worn on him as much as it had his partner. The chill of the outpost was felt heavily. He could see a small bit of yellow pollen on the windowsill from his orchid, so he hastily wiped it up with a sanitizing wipe and moved the flower to the top of the bookshelf.

He knew his lover missed flowers, but he hated the thought of the blooms killing them with something as microscopic as a spec of pollen. His eyes were drawn to the small black urn tucked up by his collection of westerns, one with stars and planets painted along its surface. A tiny container for his tiny supernova, the reason he proposed this insane idea in the first place. It was entirely his fault, London was too desperate to leave the pain behind and willingly followed him into the throes of the universe on a whim and a falsified promise.

He ruined their life.

Soft footsteps interrupted his musing thoughts. He gazed over his shoulder and felt the edge of his lips curl into a smile. London stood there, hands clasped sheepishly together. They looked at him with a contemplative stare before they approached.

"Lon—"

His thought was interrupted by a fierce and passionate kiss. He set his hands upon their waist and pulled them close.

"I need you to make me forget it all, Temp. For a moment, I need a moment," London whispered with desperation dripping from their tone.

"Pardon?"

"I need you," they set their hand on the inside of his thigh, "to help me *forget*, Temple."

Temple's brow furrowed. He kissed their forehead and closed his eyes in thought as he wrestled with the ramifications of such an intense deed amidst the height of such terrors. He nodded and grabbed their thighs, lifted their body up with a powerful, yet gentle force.

They wrapped their arms firmly around his neck and set their forehead against his. Their accelerated, desperate breathing caused a quick onset of arousal within him. A cocktail of primal desire and pure desperation to do as they asked quickly intoxicated his body.

"Of course," he cooed.

The immediate relief that hit London from his agreement was prominent. Temple was barely able to compensate for how slack their frame went; he nearly dropped them. For a moment, he thought they passed out, but the manner in which they pressed their fingertips into his skull told him that their body was simply succumbing to the hormones, the stress, and the desire. Relenting itself over to his hands.

They trusted him. Fully.

They were so foolish. And yet...

His hand slid up their spine, his fingers traced the ridges of their vertebrae. He could feel their flesh tense beneath his palm, sensitive and chilled. His lips met the curve of their jaw, and a sigh escaped their lips. Temple's breath was warm against them, it smelled of coffee. They could feel the shudder of his inhale as he suckled their skin. He craved it as deeply as they did.

It was an urgent, fearful sensation, as if they both worried it would be their last.

Temple carefully set them on the bed. He held their face in his hands, playfully squished their cheeks, and chuckled. London giggled, but the dreamy, soft look in their eyes caused his heart to skip a beat with intensity. He carefully removed their glasses and took in their features, the reddish color of their cheeks, the shimmer against their teary irises. His eyes never left their face as he opened the nightstand to retrieve a box of rubbers.

"Of all the wonders my eyes have seen, nothing compares to you," he said gently.

"You're ridiculous," they said with a sheepish laugh.

"I'm honest. Let me make slow love to you," Temple slid his hand down their waist to their leg, "Let me hold you, London."

London set the back of their hand against their mouth in embarrassment and nodded softly. They watched their husband pull the shirt from his body and toss it to the ground. His muscular arms and broad shoulders flooded their senses with an overwhelming and powerful wave of security. He knelt slowly, situated himself between their legs. Not once did his hand leave their thigh, their knee, their calf as he traced his fingers across their form. He gripped hold of their ankle and kissed the side of their foot.

Temple grabbed the waistband of their lounge pants and tenderly slid the garment down their body. With slow, methodical motions, he shifted their legs over his shoulders and pulled them forward. London eagerly awaited the moment where his lips met their flesh, nervous and embarrassed as if they had not done this a thousand times before. It still thrilled them, and they loved that sweet moment of connection. They stared at the ceiling and gasped as he made contact. Their legs shifted and compressed around his skull, their eyes fluttered closed, and they relented themself over to his mouth and the pressure of his fingers against their thighs.

His hands were powerful, a strength akin to Atlas' desperation to hold the world up. He kept their frame aloft and lifted them out of the dredges of hell with one motion. They felt alive again. They felt human. It scared them, but they craved it, and their overloaded mind did not allow them the courtesy of processing it before it shut down to accept the situation.

With a heavily shuddered breath, their back arched and their trembling hands dug valleys into his skin. Their thoughts spun mercilessly until they vanished like a dissipating storm, leaving an empty nothingness that was a welcome reprieve. A throaty moan crawled itself out of their mouth.

Sweat began to form on their brow.

Yes, this was what they needed.

A release. Warmth. Contact.

Temple slid his hands up to their waist as he followed the motions London's body while they laid back against the cold mattress. He kissed them fiercely as their legs wrapped around his torso and compressed against his ribcage. They felt the rattle of his bones and lungs against them with earthquake-like intensity as he panted with the fervor of a starving animal on the prowl. The sensation of life against their thighs was powerful.

London grabbed hold of Temple's head and bit his lower lip. They exhaled the full heat of an inferno into his lungs.

They felt him, felt his arousal press harshly into their flesh. An involuntary gasp raced out of their throat, eliciting a tender, deep laugh from their husband. London's nails clawed tracks into his shoulder blades as his free hand fumbled the ties of his sweatpants. They became but vines, desperately weaving themself into the muscular landscape of his flesh in an attempt to root to something real, something not of metal or plastic.

Temple licked his lips as London removed their shirt. He stared at their frame, at the heavy scarring across their chest from surgeries both necessary and vital. Ones that kept them alive. Ones that allowed them to be who they were meant to be. To live, to breathe and persevere. The ridges and ravines that traced across their pale flesh captivated him. He could not believe he was allowed to love them through it all.

"You are just as lovely as you were when I first saw you in that morgue all those years ago," Temple said tenderly as he kissed the side of their head. "Even more so."

"Temple…"

"I love you."

Freed of his bonds of cotton, he slowly thrusted against them and grunted fiercely as they connected. London, tears of relief, of worry, and desperation rolling down their cheeks, cried out in pleasure. They locked gazes, stilled for a brief moment, and let their lips meet as they found a comfortable place to lie. He cradled the small of their back with his palm and watched them finally succumb to the release.

The relaxed expression that overcame their face was haunting. He was haunted by a pale specter, and he welcomed the possession with open arms.

V

Naked and sprawled across the mattress, London lay atop Temple's body with little energy in their frame. Limp, their arm hung over the edge of the bed, and their head rested heavily on his chest. Their hair was knotted, oily, and hung waywardly over their sleep-heavy eyes. The rush was too much. They had no earthly idea of how long they went at it, how many times they had done it. Despite it all, for the first time in a long while they felt relaxed. Even the relentless chill and isolation of the outpost could not dampen the feeling of safety.

They were nearly dead to the universe, and Temple was grateful. He set his hand against their back and held them firmly with a desperation unlike anything they had ever felt before. London savored every precious second, but the realization that he was leaving soon hit them rapidly, relentlessly, and began turning their stomach inside of their abdomen. A small yawn overwhelmed their mouth, so they buried their face into his chest and honed in on the aggressive thump of his heart to calm their nerves.

"I'm surprised your console hasn't gone off with an ungodly amount of messages," Temple noted gently. The pull of sleep tugged on his mind with relentless intensity.

"I didn't send the report," London mumbled, losing out to their exhaustion.

Temple looked down at them with worry. "Why not?"

London pressed their face into his pectoral, an attempt at dissolving eye contact. They were nervous. Scared and unsettled.

"If they knew... what they delivered, if they knew of the horrors we burned, they'd drag you away early, Temple. It could cancel another colony attempt, which means they'll have to start over, and you'll be gone too long. I couldn't... I couldn't stand the thought of that."

"We need to send that report."

"No!" London snapped.

Temple cupped their cheek, "London... people will die if we don't. It's alright."

"I don't want you to leave me!"

"Let me handle it. I won't let them take me from you, but we need to do this."

London's frail mental state couldn't handle his determination. Sobbing, their hands trembled against him, and pained cries escaped their lips as they begged him to reconsider. Temple wrapped them up in his arms and hushed them, holding them through the moment of panic. It felt as if every word out of his mouth only brought them pain. They lingered on a precipice that would not be left easily, and every sentence he uttered pushed them closer and closer to the edge.

He hated to do this, hated to bring such distress to their system, but he couldn't rightfully go about his day refusing to inform their superiors of the possible threat, especially when his own team often handled similar situations, in similarly dangerous unknowns. People needed to be alerted, and he couldn't allow that risk to continue without warning. In a way, he knew London couldn't either.

The time to act was limited. London was notoriously thorough, notoriously quick. If an update didn't hit their employer's desk soon, people would notice and come knocking. The sharp embalmer had built a reputation of efficiency, and a delayed report would raise suspicion.

Temple smiled. "I'll be right back. Dry your eyes."

London finally pushed him away. They pulled the sheet up to their chest and turned to face the window. Tears streamed down their cheeks, and Temple's attempt at wiping them away was met with resistance. He decided to leave them be.

Throwing his clothes back on, Temple quickly moved to the office on the far end of the hall. He woke the console and was met with the results of his panels, something he had forgotten about in the throes of passion. A few red warning symbols appeared near his readings, noting a dangerous decline in his well-being that he currently didn't have the time to address, so he sent them to his personal report portal and deleted them before London could see. He tossed the vials into the hazmat bin in the corner.

He began drafting a report to attach to the autopsy notes London wrote, sprucing up the shaken grammar written during their panic. Noting the results of the autopsy, the strange anomalies found beneath the flesh of the woman, and the urgency of the matter to call off that mining project, he emphasized the fact that a proper understanding of the situation would be needed to continue digging deeper into Elysium.

He firmly stated that the body needed to be burned in an attempt at keeping London safe from the reprimands of using the oven instead of returning the corpse to the officials, and the contaminated items on the victim's person were sealed and awaiting pickup. Most importantly, he recommended finding someone specializing in parasitic organisms to handle the research, suggesting Elizabeth Fontaine, long-time girlfriend of his trusted researcher Hitomi and notorious fanatic when it came to the strangest parts of the universe. If Liza could not find an answer, she would find someone who could before anyone else in the Project could even blink.

Then, he washed his hands of the situation and hoped that he had done enough to save some lives. As he sat in the small office, listening to the sound of the hydroponics stations whirring around him, he found himself yawning. The week had exhausted him. He felt as if he were only hindering his lover's mental stability and that his own much needed time to rest was dwindling with the need to care for them. He didn't mind, but he felt helpless.

"I'm going back to bed after I check on the oven. You don't need to say goodbye," London said firmly from the doorway. One of their shawl-collared sweaters had been draped over their body, and an air of anger and anxiety radiated off them with the intensity of the sun.

Temple turned to address them. "I'm not going anywhere."

"Don't be an idiot, Temple. You just gave them the all-clear to pull you back to duty. You have an hour, tops, before—"

The console screen flickered with the notification of an incoming message. Temple exhaled angrily and answered the correspondence. It was only a call, meaning it was someone with power in the Project, someone too important to feel the need to show their face. It meant trouble.

"Captain Davies reporting," Temple stated calmly.

"Just the man I was looking for. I received Doctor Davies' report. Apologies for causing such a ruckus with that corpse. We didn't realize the direness of the situation, but we appreciate the thorough examination despite the unknown of it all. Hopefully, they're well? We were... concerned with the delay," the hidden voice inquired cooly.

The Davies knew it well. It was grating and haunted their lives like a relentless ghost in the machine that kept them afloat. It was not one that spoke with friendliness in her tone. Her inflection was stone cold, feigning empathy and concern in an attempt at masking the morbid curiosity that dripped from her tongue. She was a cruel individual who oversaw her employees with an iron fist and strong sense of urgency—Doctor Nikita Romanov, head of the Developmental Sciences Department, and someone Temple disliked with a passion.

Like hell she read it. The turnaround was too quick. She was waiting for the report.

"I'm fine, Doctor Romanov. I was just about to tell Captain Davies goodbye and see if he needed lunch before he left," London replied in a monotone, tired voice.

"London—"

"Always so efficient. That's why we entrust these serious cases to you. Even with your *disabilities* and limitations, you're the best embalmer we have. We happen to have a transport vessel in the area with another corpse that came from a nearby site a few kilos away from the one you just handled. They will pick up Captain Davies on their way back—"

"My leave isn't over, Doctor Romanov," Temple reminded.

"And yet progress and time moves onward, Captain. This new... issue, along with this second death in such a close proximity has forced the expedition to be halted *temporarily* on Elysium, so we need your team to resume its work. We've lost valuable time because of this, and time is a commodity that we cannot afford to waste any more of," Romanov stated firmly.

"The drill is broken," Temple continued.

"A minor setback," she replied.

"I need to be here. I promised London I would be here."

"And you promised humanity that you would find them a new home. Doctor Davies will understand. It's part of the job. Be ready to depart within the half hour. Thank you both for your service."

The call ended. Temple slammed his fist down on the console. A surge of sharp, agonizing pain shot through his hand, but he couldn't acknowledge it, not with London's eyes lingering. He finally sat up straight and turned the chair to face them.

They stood expressionless, broken, and betrayed.

"London, I'm sorry," Temple apologized.

They simply turned and walked back down the corridor. Temple stood and followed with long strides, begging for them to acknowledge him. He knew that look, that sudden sense of silence and distance in their gaze. They were dissociating. He couldn't leave them like this.

Tenderly, he snatched up their arm as they headed into the bedroom. "London, don't do this. Please."

"Do what, Temple? Be upset that you didn't listen to me? That you did exactly what you always do when you come home from leave?"

"And what is that, London?"

"You sweet talk me with falsified words of hope and build me up just to rip it all out from under me by walking out that door before you should. You come home when it's convenient and you need to fuck, then it's right back to business, back to doing everything those assholes ask of you without question. The moment they come calling, I stop mattering to you. You'll be gone another, what, four... six months this time? They'll have to start over again because of this. That's a lifetime here, Temple, and I'd rather it be alone than believe things will change—believe you love me enough to change."

Temple gritted his teeth and bit his tongue to stop himself from interrupting or snapping at them. He knew it was their stress talking. At least, he hoped it was the stress. His heart couldn't handle the thought of them believing those words to be true. They were too intelligent for reasoning such as that, especially when they were the one who begged him to take them to bed only a few hours prior.

It made him realize how they saw his interactions since this nightmare of an endeavor started. How little else they had to occupy their time when those brief days of leave would come and go so rapidly. The majority of his days off had been spent in bed, and they would notice it more than he would. He'd head back to work and find distractions. They had to sit in this damned box and contemplate it. He made a mess of things, and he didn't know if he could rectify it.

"Don't come back, Temple," London stated as they set their hand atop his.

"This is my home, and I love you. I'll come back as soon as I can," Temple promised.

"I don't…" they hesitated, "I think it would be best if you focused on your job. Don't come back."

Temple finally released his hold on their arm. They fixed their sleeves and continued into the bedroom with the intent of packing up his belongings. That was a finality he wasn't prepared to accept. Anything that left the outpost could not come back, not with the high level of irritants that would stitch themselves into his garments. He came and went naked as the day he was born. Uniforms remained aboard his ship while his civilian clothes hung hardly worn in the closet. A packed shelf of books sat well-loved in his office while a small collection of stories remained unread in the bedroom he shared with his lover.

It was a duality of lives lived to keep them safe. The two could not intermingle. It was a death sentence for them, one they were well aware of, and the fact they had given up so thoroughly broke him.

He watched them sternly, leaning on the doorway to not only block their ability to leave but make himself vulnerable and visible to them. Wordlessly, he studied their every move as they found a metal crate in the closet and began pulling his clothes from their hangers.

Even in their anger, they folded each garment with care. Even in their rage, they still loved him enough to handle the details with a tender touch.

"Where else am I to go, London?" Temple inquired after half his clothes had been packed. He waited for them to speak, but they remained silent, so he needed to intervene.

"This new frontier you're so desperate to find," London replied quietly.

"That's not why I'm here, London. That's not why I came to this place."

"Then you'd best find what it is you're truly looking for, Temple, because I don't think you'll find it here. Not anymore."

"I don't know what else I can do to convince you that everything I've done is for you. I think you know it, but it can't be easy remembering it when I do little to prove it, when you associate my leaving with a lack of love and desire. It isn't true. I leave because I have to—"

"You don't!"

"I do!" Temple barked, only to quickly fix his posture and tone when he saw his lover tense. "I do. You have *no* idea what it's like out there, London. And I don't mean to be harsh with those words or imply that you're naive. I know you'd rather be out there with us, with me, but it is brutal and unforgiving in a way you can't fathom. You are safe here. If you leave... you will die, and that means I have to do everything in my power to ensure this outpost remains in your hands. If I rebel, fight back, or refuse orders, this place is at risk, and so are you. You know that. My hands are tied if I want you safe and in a sterile environment where you can live. If I could be here, I would... I simply can't."

London quietly sniffled as they approached the bookshelf to pull Temple's novels from the collection. Their eyes locked onto their son's urn, peppered with tiny stars, and the reality of their horrid life settled in again. How they yearned for this all to be over.

"I'm not taking that crate," Temple said firmly as he approached. He didn't touch them, but he needed to be close.

"I can't do this anymore," London admitted.

"Then I will find a way to make this my last trip."

"They own you, and I don't think you're willing to do what you have to for that to change."

"What is protocol?"

London swallowed hard.

"What is protocol for permanent removal from a mission that won't jeopardize what we have here? What is damaging enough? Impactful enough? Tell me what it is, and I will make it happen," Temple promised.

London weakly shook their head.

No. How could he? That would be an impossible ask, a selfish and problematic ask, and they could not bear the weight of the responsibility. He needed to live, they needed him to live, even if he did so without them in his narrative. Still, his tender, worried touch against their arm left them contemplating the possibilities.

The shrill tone of the door sensor rang out through the outpost. His transport had arrived. A new, possibly dangerous body had arrived. Their time was over, snuffed out like a nova bursting, leaving only a black hole to swallow them with relentless remorse.

"Find out what I need to do; make sure it's encrypted. I'll come home to you," he promised as he set his hand beneath their chin. He softly nudged their misty eyes up toward him, allowing them to gaze into his strong, unwavering eyes that were half hidden by a smile. He was confident in this. It frightened them.

They believed him.

"I love you," Temple said confidently.

They hadn't the heart to say it back, to re-open the connection that they tried so hard to sever. Though their lips did part to say it, and that was enough. He knew they did. He was not angered or upset by the fact they could not return the sentiment aloud.

He kissed them briefly, so as not exacerbate the emotions in the outpost. It was only as they leaned into it that he felt as if he managed to pull them back from the ledge they decided to build their home upon.

"The loss of limb, a terminal diagnosis, or absolute failure of a psych eval," London mumbled as the angry chime of the bay door rang again. "Those are your options per the Project's safety protocol. The biggest need would be still proving yourself worthwhile afterward if we want to keep the outpost. You'd need to be useless for their cause but still vital enough to keep alive. Otherwise, you'd be disposed of without much thought."

"I'll call you tonight," Temple promised.

"Don't come home unless you plan on staying, Temple."

Temple nodded firmly. They believed him. He was determined to make sure this trip was his last, and they were afraid of the state he'd return to them in. Afraid of how he'd drag his team into whatever heinous plan he'd concoct, of how dedicated they were and how easily they'd oblige him in his possibly suicidal endeavors.

He kissed their cheek and headed for the door, making a firm and boisterous statement by not retrieving any of his items as he went. That cocky ego of his. They hated how endearing it was, how deeply they believed and loved him.

London followed him to the front door with an emotionless visage washed in the hue of the grow lights around them. They watched the motions of his shoulder blades as he pulled his shirt from his body, the strong definition that cut through his dark flesh and the surety of movements. They could see the war wounds made in the midst of love, broken skin ripped from their nails and the desperation in the way they clung to him.

"Burn the body, London," Temple stated.

"Pardon?"

"Burn the body. It isn't worth the risk. Feed them the lies they want, but don't open that corpse. You are too valuable to lose over their madness, and this smells vile," he demanded as he turned to look back at them. It had been far too long since they had seen that sense of pure, utter seriousness in his gaze. All they could do was nod.

Temple opened the bay and stopped dead in his tracks upon seeing two individuals clad in regulation spacesuits standing there, helmets removed, and the docking tunnel to their ship wide open behind them. An angered scowl crested his face.

"You can't be in here!" Temple barked.

"We have orders, sir," one of the grunts replied, tone apologetic and worried. The young woman at his side stepped back out of fear.

"Get the fuck out! *Now!*" Temple snapped.

"Sir—"

London gasped. They grabbed their chest and wheezed. A small trickle of blood ran down their chin, through their gritted teeth, over their trembling lip. Temple turned back to look at them with concern, but they hastily placed their hands against his spine and pushed, urging him to go so they could seal up the outpost. The intensity of their wounds caused such a sharp, immediate reaction, and it frightened him. Even with the distance, something in the newly arrived ship throttled the air in their lungs. It was so quick, so fatal.

"London!"

He could see the tears in their eyes as their hands extended to input the security code, to shut the bay door. Temple stepped back into the chill of the decontamination chamber, understanding the frantic need, and watched as their frame disappeared behind the door halves as they slammed shut. The last he saw of his partner was them coughing blood out onto the floor. They mouthed a soft *I love you* and vanished from sight.

Temple slammed his fist against the wall. One of the grunts spoke to him, attempted to touch his arm. Blinded by rage, Temple snapped his hand back and grabbed the pilot's frail neck, bundling his flesh up like a paper to be crumpled. He wanted to break him, wanted to crush his vertebrae and feel the life leave his body for what he did, what this damn expedition and those who felt as if they owned him did.

Seeing the fear in the young woman's eyes at his side forced him to stop. The universe didn't need any further bloodshed. He didn't need to be locked up. He relented and dropped the transport pilot to the floor, leaving the young man frantically gasping for breath with terror in his expression.

"I need to detox the bay because of your stupidity. Leave," Temple demanded.

The woman snatched up her companion and helped escort him to the transport ship. Temple waited until he was alone to fully strip down and wash his body before he stepped into his spacesuit. He wanted to open that door, to ensure his lover was safe, but it was too risky. Too many eyes could see that code, too many bodies could wander back into the bay, dragging particles and pollen into his home. He also knew London could not handle him returning, that the outpost was being detoxed, and they needed time to adjust to this new nightmare.

He would be home soon enough, even if it killed him.

VI

A full day cycle had come and gone, and Temple still had not heard from London. They ignored every attempted call, message, and chat request through the reporting app he sent them. No news had come of the second autopsy, leaving many to wonder what had happened to the infamous London Davies after their husband was swiftly ripped away from them. The only solace the research crew of the Gibraltar outpost could find was that no statement had been released, so they could rest easy knowing the embalmer was alive.

So long as a body was in their care, someone would come looking if the silence lingered too long.

Temple's team was on edge. Their love and admiration for London was notorious. They all felt the loss of their presence among them, and the found family and bonded crew could sense the anger and worry coming from their captain as he waited for news. The entire situation was farcical, fabricated to pull Temple from his leave early. Despite the chaotic and rushed return to duty, they spent the last twenty-six hours aboard their ship without clearance to land on Gibraltar to continue the research that was deemed so crucial and timely it upended the entire crew's much needed leave.

Temple and his most trusted employees locked themselves away in the captain's quarters and contemplated the situation while the rest of the team tried to find ways to pass the time elsewhere on the vessel.

"This is bollocks," Matthias, the team's data analyst and Temple's admin, noted as he crossed his legs atop the captain's desk.

Chopsticks in hand, he pulled at the steaming, bland noodles in his bowl and took a small bite. His appetite was failing him after he heard the reports of what happened to the miner on Elysium. It had been failing him for a while, but he'd never admit it aloud, and the wriggling black unknowns inside of the dusty corpse left his nausea at an all-time high. Temple felt it best his team knew. They were too loyal for him to deny them the knowledge of these strange new developments.

Still, Matthias needed to eat. His meds demanded it, so he forced himself to swallow despite the uncomfortable similarity of his food's motions to the monstrosities that sucked the poor miner dry.

His blue eyes were tired-looking behind his smudged glasses. His oily, dirty blonde hair was pushed back with a headband, and he was in desperate need of a shave. He looked ragged, his nail polish was chipped, and his lips were dried. The stomach bug that had been ailing him since his first day of leave seemed to be settling in for the long haul.

"Which part?" Hitomi inquired as she looked at her tablet.

She was hours deep into a novel, waiting for soil samples to process and provide some answers to the madness. Her girlfriend, stationed far away in the orbit of Elysium, was in the process of studying the contents of the parasite-ridden miner's biohazard bin, and she missed her dearly. She wondered what her partner's research was showing. Per Temple's request, Hitomi asked her partner if she could dig into the strange happenings and report back with discretion, and they were all impatiently waiting for the results. The sudden halting of progress on the soon-to-be-failed colony left many research teams uneasy.

It felt as if all they had done as of late was wait.

Damn it all to hell, she was bored. Her long, hot-pink-dyed hair was pinned to the back of her head, wound up in a meticulously done braid without a single strand out of place. The numerous piercings across her face and ears caught the light of the irritatingly bright bulb above them. A fresh strip of bleach rested on her roots, processing much too slowly for her liking. She was in desperate want of a shower.

Matthias threw his arms out. "All of it. This is bollocks. We have no reason to be out here right now. We can't even work. The drill's broken, we don't have an all-clear from the safety team so we don't know when we can return to the surface, and even then it's not like we can really do much. This was all a ruse because Doctor Romanov got a hair up her arse—"

"Matthias, please," Temple begged. "Now's not the time, nor the place, for conversations as such. Take this as a learning opportunity to understand why discretion is important, especially when the walls can listen to you." His tone was soaked in parental understanding and empathy.

"Sorry, Cap, I'm pissed. I'm worried about Doctor Davies," Matthias said sheepishly.

"I'm sure they're fine. They're the toughest person in the Project even if they refuse to believe it themself. I'm sure they need some time to process. You know how they get," Hitomi replied firmly as she shut off her tablet.

"Still, two flare-ups in a week has to be hard to recover from. I know that purge medication is rough on their stomach, too. I just hope they're eating and getting some sleep. They'll call when they're ready, they always do, but they have to be feeling so sick and scared," Matthias mused.

Hitomi shot him an angered glance, wishing he would find a way to hold his tongue and stop adding fuel to the fire. She knew he meant well, but his inability to censor his thoughts and the brazen opinions of his youth often caused more problems than needed. Still, the harsh cough that escaped his lungs and the grimace that shot across his face caused her to bite her tongue. He was young and plucky, he didn't know any better, and it was obvious he was unwell.

"He's right, Temple. I'm sure they're fine. They need some time to let their body recover. I bet they're curled up in bed with a glass of wine and a good book," Hitomi added, tone sure and confident.

"I'm mostly concerned about that second corpse, in all honesty. London is allowed to be upset and angry. I haven't given them a reason to be anything other than furious with me. I'm more afraid that they would try and use that new project as a way to de-stress and they might overdo it or miss something vital and end up hurt despite the fact that I told them to burn the body immediately. I'm... jarred by the things I saw in the lab, that's all," Temple noted.

"Can I see that footage again?" Hitomi requested.

Temple nodded and grabbed his tablet. Out of precaution, he had sent the report and recordings to himself to use as leverage. He needed irrefutable proof in case something happened because of this new development, especially to his partner. It would be easy for this to be swept under the rug, for it to turn to lies while countless more suffer from that same negligence. He wondered how many more individuals may have already been infected, how many parasites managed to crawl into hosts and burrow deep into the last living members of humanity. As selfish as it was, he was thankful he was far away from Elysium.

Time felt limited, as if it were dwindling in excess and humankind was on its way to demise at the hands of something unimaginable. It made Temple wish he was home.

Hitomi took the device and looked at the recording of the black worms as they crawled through the corpse in high-def quality. She tightened her grip, furrowed her thinly plucked eyebrows, and began gnawing on her lip rings.

"I hope Liza is okay," she mumbled.

"You gave her enough of a heads up to be mindful, right?" Matthias asked quietly.

"Yes," she replied.

"Make sure you call her later to be sure. I can't imagine those things could survive without a host, but we don't know what's in the soil or debris that made it onto the miner's gear, how they reproduce, what other variants may look like. I don't want Liza infected," Temple said with a heavy sigh.

Matthias pressed his hand against his mouth and gagged. The chopsticks in his grip trembled aggressively with the unsteadiness of his fingers. Temple noticed. He saw how slack his young admin's shoulders were and how pale he seemed. Sweat rolled down the side of his face, along his jaw, dripping into his bowl of noodles.

"Are you still running a fever?" Temple inquired.

"A bit," Matthias replied as he set his dish to the side. He slid his hands into the pocket of his oversized sweatshirt and shivered.

"Go to bed."

"Captain—"

"Matthias, go to bed. That's an order. We aren't leaving the ship anytime soon, and I don't need you getting worse. Your glucose readings are still high, and you know how hard it is for you to recover from spikes that bad."

Matthias blinked his eyes unevenly, as if he struggled to process what the captain told him. Temple stood and approached. He set the back of his hand against Matthias' forehead.

"You're burning up. Did they give you a diagnosis?" Temple inquired.

"No," Matthias whispered. "I just grabbed some meds from a quick-hop clinic on *The Olympia* before I left. They told me to eat in small doses, so I'm trying, but... it hurts. It feels more like muscle cramps than the flu. My abdomen is aching... So is my low back."

Temple helped ease Matthias off the desk. He could feel how unsteady his body was, how warm he felt. Every motion seemed to cause an ache. A pained exhale slipped through his gritted teeth.

"Let's get you to bed," Temple urged.

"No, I'm fine," Matthias whimpered.

"You haven't slept since we got back. You won't kick that virus if you keep running yourself ragged," Hitomi reminded with an inquisitive eyebrow cocked high. She noticed he seemed on edge. It was an unusual thing for the usually chipper lad.

"She's right, you need the rest. I'll come get you if I need you," Temple assured.

"I'm scared to be alone, Cap," Matthias finally admitted.

Temple set his hand against Matthias' back to help stabilize him, "Come lay down," he urged as he escorted him to his own bed.

Matthias tensed a bit in rebellion, but he was too weak to argue. The mattress was cold against his palm as he fumbled for a seat. Temple never once let his fingers leave his admin's body until he was sure he was stable.

"I don't want to get you sick," Matthias said quietly.

"You've been in my room for hours now, kiddo. Too late for those worries now. Just rest. You're safe here. My immune system is strong enough," Temple assured.

Matthias looked back at him. His eyelids were reddened, and his skin was slick with sweat. A heavy set of breaths showcased a shudder of his chest, visible beneath the heavy cotton of his Zeus Project sweatshirt. He seemed to struggle to breathe in a meaningful way. The admin winced and coughed again.

The heavy thump of the spaceship around them became dulled as the captain slid a pair of headphones over his head. Gentle, soothing music began to play. The rattling pain in Matthias' skull softened as the droning agony of the environment around him became muted, as his motion sickness quelled with something else to hone onto. Tears welled in his eyes, so Temple pulled the headphones back so he could speak to him.

"Should I take you to the med bay?" he asked.

"I just need some sleep, Cap," he assured.

"Then sleep as long as you need. We'll keep our voices down."

Matthias nodded and laid down atop the mattress, fixing the headphones as he went. Temple, hoping to help him sweat out the fever, pulled a quilt over his body and returned to his office chair. He watched the young man quickly fall asleep to the soft sound of wind instruments.

Hitomi, still studying the footage of the body London processed the day prior, paid little mind to the conversation. She only moved her eyes to her superior when she saw the unmistakable slackening of Matthias' body as he gave in to his exhaustion. Still, she held the tablet tight in her grip and searched for the words she wanted to say.

She had known Temple for decades, watched him grow from an awkward research assistant to a proud, confident leader amongst his peers. One vibrant and beloved enough to cause dozens of scientists and researchers to join the Zeus Project without hesitation. He was an explorer at heart; he yearned for adventure and the thrill of discovery. It was at war with his devotion to his partner, at war with his tiring mind. He was a spaceman cemented to a ship, unable to step out among the stars and unable to go home. He was trapped like a bug in a cup.

Hitomi watched him fall in love with London, watched him grieve the loss of his son. She even agreed to give up everything to follow him to the darkest reaches of the galaxy after her own career and life collapsed around her. Temple was her trusted friend—her only friend—and the prospect of an endless universe to explore at his side was an easy one to accept. She didn't regret it, but she hated how things fell apart once they woke from cryo-sleep. The lack of London's presence hit the group hard; she missed them, and she could tell Temple was growing more unsettled by the day as the distance and stars between them extended.

With so much life lived by his side, she could easily see that he was overwhelmed, that Matthias' health was concerning him more than he'd openly say. She didn't want to upset him, but she needed to put her foot down.

"You should stop coddling him," Hitomi said quietly.

"I'm not," Temple shot back, keeping his tone soft.

"You are. He shouldn't be afraid to sleep in his own damn room. You need to let him face those fears."

"He's allowed to be worried, and he's still practically a child—especially compared to us. None of this is going how he planned. He was promised a position beside London in a cozy lab with things to do and greenery to ease his mind. He came because of London, and now he's stuck here in this cold ship tending to the little tasks I can give him. He's also incredibly sick. I want him nearby so I can keep an eye on him. You know how neglectful he is of his numbers when he's ill. If he's throwing up, his insulin he needs to be monitored."

"We should *all* be in a warm outpost keeping our hands busy, that's not the point. He's never going to overcome his anxiety, or learn to manage his health, if you don't let him face it."

Temple looked at her with a bit of contempt that turned to understanding. She was, of course, right. Still, he couldn't help but worry. Matthias was a shining, young genius who willingly followed London into this madness out of loyalty and devotion. After interning with them in his final year of high school, the young man fell in love with the process of fixing up bodies and begged them to come along on this new project in the vastness of space.

Hard as London tried to dissuade him, Matthias' mind was set, and he gave up everything at the young age of eighteen for a broken promise and an absolute hellscape of lies. A late-stage diagnosis of juvenile diabetes straight out of cryo-sleep didn't help.

Still, he tried to keep his chin up and be strong. He worked diligently to aid Temple, but the captain could tell that he was getting tired of the infrequent, quick bursts of chaos and long droning days of nothing to do. The sudden uptick of bodies and strange occurrences that began appearing among the other research and development teams didn't help.

"I know you feel responsible for him—"

"I *am* responsible for him," Temple interrupted. "And I owe it to London to keep him safe. That's what I'm doing. I don't want him to lose that spark of joy and wonder he has. He's not corrupted and cranky like us old folks are. As soon as I get his transfer cleared and have him move in with London, I'll stop worrying. It's just taking much longer than I'd like. They can't keep denying it when both of them keep declining health-wise. Zeus will cave one day. London needs an aide, too. Especially if the bodies keep coming as frequently as they are."

Hitomi sighed and set her head in her hand. She studied Temple's expression, how his gaze never drifted from Matthias' back. With a judgment-filled motion, she turned the tablet around.

"How about you? Huh? *Is* your immune system strong enough? How about *your* health?" she said accusingly, putting so much emphasis on her words he felt she might burst a blood vessel.

His panel report was lit up across the tablet screen. The bright red warning symbols had not been forgotten, but he hadn't been given a moment of privacy to study them. His two most trusted employees had remained close by since they re-boarded their research vessel. He didn't mind, he preferred it, but his personal matters had not been tended to.

"I don't know, I haven't looked at them yet. You two won't leave me alone long enough to figure out if I'm dying," Temple chided.

"Should I send it to Liza?" Hitomi inquired.

"Would you? I feel fine other than some excess fatigue, but those numbers are concerning. I'm a rock and earth and soil guy, not a body guy. They mean nothing to me, and I don't want to miss something vital."

"Didn't London say anything?"

"I deleted the report before they could see it."

"This is why they're struggling, Temple. They can't trust you to be honest because you aren't. You're too protective of them, both of them, and it's not helping either of their constitutions or anxiety levels. They're not children."

"Can I trust you to send those panels to Liza?"

Hitomi sighed and nodded. There would be no arguing with him, not when he got like this. She saw his broad shoulders release some of their tension and knew the conversation was over. So, she stood and handed his tablet back to him before she patted his shoulder, excusing herself from the conversation before she grew more frustrated.

"Get some rest, Temp, you're looking tired," Hitomi stated. It was a demand.

"You, too. Say hello to Liza for me. Tell her to keep her chin up," Temple said with his signature, confident grin.

"I will. Let me know if London calls. I'll be in the washroom if you need me."

The researcher exited out into the bright, blinding hallway. The door slid shut behind her and draped the room in a heavy quiet. He laid his head back against the chair and listened to the humming, technologically-induced quiet of the ship. It was a unique lack of sound, mostly ambient and ghostly, as if it didn't actually exist but still haunted the world around him. He pondered the journeys of the ghosts that wandered through the machines, wondered what it was they found so intriguing about this particular place in the galaxy and the fools who wrecked it with their greed.

He unlocked his tablet as he slid over to his desk, deciding to use the moment of quiet to look into something that had been plaguing his mind. Remotely, he logged into the outpost cameras and scrubbed back through the feeds to try and find the moments the door chimes rang out with seemingly no one at the door. His plan was to look into them before breakfast the day prior, but the unexpected miner had halted his good intentions.

The footage was spotty once he bypassed the brief handful of days he had been in the outpost. With little movement in the lower floors, most of the timeline was blank. With how sterile the building was, the cameras rarely even found a speck to hone in on, so they remained in their stand-by modes the majority of the time. He found the moment a few weeks prior when London tended to the McCalls' daughter and used that as the beginning of the period he needed to research.

He leaned forward and began searching for blips in the black bars along the screen. The lab-level loading bay door opened a few hours after the small girl was processed. A woman in a spacesuit came to retrieve the small bag containing the ashes London placed there earlier.

The lab lights only turned on briefly a few days after when London came back down to drop a small bit of artificial meat into Silas' container. They sat for a few minutes and watched the parasite's sharpened, long legs puncture the chicken with aggression, then the yawning embalmer retreated back upstairs. Nothing else happened on the second floor until two weeks later when Temple's team offloaded the grocery crates.

He switched to the morgue cameras. The pitch-black room, unvisited for months until Temple went down to check for bodies, seemed to have one too many camera activations for his liking. The lights never turned on, but the cameras did. It caught *something*, even if he could not see what that something was. He studied each recording closely and found no bits of dust or debris, so he felt confident in knowing that the fungal half-corpse was safely contained.

As much as he disliked Liza's project germinating in his basement, he saw no true issues with it in regard to London's health. The case seemed to contain it properly. He didn't smell any mold or notice his own allergies acting up, and no visible contaminants could be seen.

The fact that he couldn't come up with a tangible reason as to why the cameras kept tripping bothered him. It seemed too rhythmic, too consistent to be a glitch. Each recording appeared to be the same number of seconds, if only differing by a minuscule amount. It wasn't until two days before his return that something tangible happened, something strange enough that his blood ran cold.

The bay door opened.

The bay door could not be opened. Not without the key code that was only known by a handful of individuals in the whole of the galaxy. But he saw it. He watched the white panel slide into the wall. He heard the keypad chime with acceptance. The lights flickered on, the entrance to the corridor that connected to the decommissioned research and medical outposts popped open, and the sound of footsteps could vaguely be heard. He swore whispers crawled out through the speakers. The same sounds he heard when he arrived home. The same sounds that London was so fearful of.

Then the feed was cut. It was the only occurrence of the door opening, and the logs reflected it, too. Still, he couldn't understand what could trip the cameras with how unbelievably sterile the outpost was. He also couldn't understand how the doors were closed when he went to check without it being caught on the video feed. It was a problem.

A soft, irritated groan exited his lips. He was too damn tired to theorize, so he convinced himself it was a system glitch until he had more clarity to tackle the issue. He turned the camera notifications on for the outpost, despite London's disdain for it. They hated the thought of him watching them, of an omniscient presence looming over their shoulders, but he needed to catch the anomalies in real time to deduce the issue. If it kept them safe, they'd find a way to forgive him.

As much as he wanted to check in on them, to see what they were doing, to see if the body had been handled, he decided against it. Hitomi's words left him contemplating his actions, his relationship. He needed to prove he was trustworthy, and allowing them their privacy and time was a good starting place. Still, he sent them one more message to let them know he loved them and turned off his console.

His dark eyes turned toward his admin. Waiting for a brief moment to ensure he didn't stir from his aggravated exhale, Temple stood and turned down the lights so he could rest his eyes. His phone remained without notifications, so he set it in his breast pocket so he could feel the vibrations if his lover finally decided to reach out.

He desperately prayed they would.

VII

The body was disgusting. London had never seen anything like it. They wondered if the delay in coming to check on it since its arrival caused the intense shifting of its form, or if the ungodly state it was in was how it had been delivered. What an unsightly color of green, what an unholy decay of its maw, what a terrifying mess its eyes had melted into. The irises, pupils, and bloodshot veins slid around inside of the corpse's goggles like oil in water, suspended in a mess of blood and brain matter that seeped out of the now unplugged eye sockets.

The jiggly shaking of it all as they wheeled it into the lab was unpleasant.

What a mess.

A fascinating, delightful mess.

When Doctor Romanov messaged to inquire about the delay in processing the deceased the afternoon prior, London told her they had not yet recovered from the last cadaver that tried to kill them and would get to it when they felt like it. Adding a passive aggressive so kindly fuck off to the end of their response, they left it at that and went to bed. What could she rightfully do to them? She had already taken so much. Nothing else mattered, and London had had enough.

They felt ill. The flare up was not as painful as the previous one, but it still caused wear on their body and a lingering nausea they weren't used to. They assumed it was some sort of dust from the ship's ventilation system, as they could smell a musty scent in the decontamination chamber before they sealed it, and their esophagus grew sensitive when their respiratory system was irritated. It made moving hard.

Their husband's relentless attempts at correspondence didn't help, either. They didn't know if they should respond. They didn't know what their heart wanted. What they did know for certain was that they needed sleep with a warm compress, so they allowed themself that pleasure and left the body to rot below them without much care for a full day before tending to it.

Despite Temple's stern warnings, they woke with a temptation to perform an autopsy. Even if they decided against it, the body needed to be transported, so they decided to make their choice once they had eyes on it. Now that they did, their curiosity overwhelmed them. They needed to know what caused this atrocity.

Unlike the previous delivery that was dried and arid, this one was moist and squishy even with the chill. It looked like a body of water attempting to replicate a human shape, flattened as if all of their innards had liquified. The gooey mess sloshed around inside of the flesh sack like a half-full water balloon. They were unsure they could even puncture it, lest they risk allowing the contaminants to spill out across the lab.

Even through their heavy hazmat gear and respiratory equipment, they could once again smell a lingering musty scent, a bit moldy but not fungal. Perhaps the odor from the transport ship originated from the corpse and it seeped out, wove itself into the environment during the long flight. They found themself curious as to what Elysium looked like, to have such drastically different cruelties in which to kill someone. It was no wonder the possible planet sat so high on the list of priorities. It must have been glorious and prosperous despite its dangers.

Out of the corner of their eye, they saw Silas shift in its terrarium. The spider-like parasite seemed to shirk away from the sight of the body, reacting to its presence in the room as they entered with the gurney. That little demon fascinated them. It was highly aware of its surroundings and a strong indicator that something was amiss.

"Hey, it's alright. You're safe," London soothed as they tapped on the glass.

Silas scratched the side of its container with slow motions, comforted by its owner's calm tone and gentle approach. After a moment tending to their caged companion, it scurried under its rock, leaving the embalmer to do their work in peace as they turned the warming light on over their desk to help the arachnid stay calm. The tube of oyster mushrooms had grown significantly since they last looked at it. They were unsure if their eyes had looked at it long enough to properly gauge the sizes during the last autopsy, but they were sure a massive amount of growth had occurred since Silas' last feeding. It didn't feel natural.

London secured the gurney next to the autopsy table and into better lighting so they could document it. Whether or not they would be slicing into it was yet to be determined, so they decided to save their strength and leave the body until it was necessary to move it. They turned on their medical tablet and hit the record button to notate their process.

"This is disgusting... London Davies, recording the observations of..." they looked at the name attached to the processing report on their terminal, "Unknown..."

How? How could there possibly be an unknown in a project that required such heavy vetting, interviews, and protocols to be allowed participation? With only a few hundred individuals in the Project, every person hired by Zeus was well known, especially by their teams, so how could no one know the name that belonged to this body?

"The victim was found near a large body of liquid on Elysium. The decedent was part of a research team of three that were tasked with taking environmental samples. The team had not checked in with their captain in over two hours, so a recovery effort was sent to investigate and found the vic lying on the edge of the basin.

"The cadaver is gangrenous looking. Every ounce of visible flesh is a unique shade of evergreen, almost blackened, but with a metallic sheen. It looks deflated, but I could hear liquid moving around inside upon transport into the lab despite it having been in deep-freeze for at least two day cycles. The uniform belongs to a ground explorer. The hiking boots are caked in a mud-like substance, and I can see clear signs of a dark, clay-like soil in the creases of the fabric. I am... unable to determine the sex of the corpse due to the collapsing of their frame and the design of their gear. All of the hair has fallen out, including the eyebrows.

"The mouth..." London set their scalpel against the dried lips, "looks almost sewn shut. It appears dried out despite the... moistness of the body. The lips are compressed so tightly that I cannot pry them open, even with the scalpel. The eyes have melted, for lack of a better term, and are floating around inside of the sealed goggles. Judging by how secure the uniform is around the body, I can only assume they were working in a hazardous environment that required them to keep their skin protected."

They leaned over the head and studied the pores atop the scalp. "The top of the head also appears dried and shriveled, as do the ears. The nasal flaps have folded in and adhered to the skin, sealing up the openings. It gives the impression that any unprotected area of flesh was impacted differently than the parts that were kept protected, leaving me to question why the majority of the head was left uncovered in the first place aside from the eyes..."

London stopped their audio recording and began snapping photos of the body. It was unusual. As if whatever had happened to this individual caused all openings to seal, possibly to ensure that something inside was protected, to keep it from leaking out. The most logical conclusion, after what they had witnessed a few days prior, was that some parasitic anomaly had taken over the body and turned it into a habitat for it to breed. Creating a sealed, moist bubble to safely reside in.

They were curious to know what was resting just beneath the flesh, beneath the uniform, but they couldn't concoct a way to open it safely. After what was found inside of the miner, they were too cautious to handle this situation in a professional manner. They needed to be human, listen to their husband, and move along. It wasn't worth the risk, but they still needed to document it and do their due diligence to save lives from the same fate and keep Zeus off of their doorstep.

As much as it angered them, Temple was right. Their job was to protect the masses, learn from the deaths that were delivered to their home, and report it. They were a scientist, and this body was the newest discovery lying in wait for their hands to document.

As they focused their camera on the head. They zoomed in to get a clear shot of the gooey mess beneath the safety goggles. They studied the eyes.

The eyes looked back.

London gasped and stepped away.

"Calm down, it's just the lighting," they mumbled to themself.

They looked at the photo they snapped and then shifted their gaze back to the body.

No. It *moved*.

The pupil was slightly higher than it was in the split-second prior when they took the photo. Their eyebrows furrowed and a shaky breath rattled their sore lungs.

Slowly, they picked up their scalpel again and tapped the glass covering over the skull. The pupil moved toward it, as if honing in on the sound. They dragged the pointed tip of their tool over the glass and studied the wild mess of eyes that swam around inside the muck like tadpoles.

"Holy... fuck," they mumbled.

They hit record on their device and captured the moment. They had no inkling as to whether or not the owner of the body was responding or if the unknown that killed it woke up now that the cold was dissipating.

A gloved finger twitched. London lowered their scalpel and took another look at the corpse. How could they check if there was a heartbeat beneath all of those protective layers? How could they know if the shifting of its chest was due to breath or the slow motions of the outpost? How could verifying life change anything?

"Can you... hear me?" London asked, voice barely a whisper.

The eyes shifted again. The skull moved slightly.

They set their glove-covered hand against the cheek, and a pained, gurgling groan rattled through the muted mouth.

"Oh... God."

They were alive. Somehow, in that messy, boggy husk, this person was alive. Or something intelligent was, at least. Panic flooded their mind. Their eyes quickly shifted to the crematorium hatch as the body began to jerk. It attempted to rise up off the gurney, but the weight of the liquid-filled mass pulled it back down. The heft of it wrapped around the skeletal system and the skin sunk against bones with such force they could see it against the skin-tight uniform, creating a grotesque mask of mismatched parts. Of life and logic fighting death and distortion.

They raced to the oven and powered it on, dropping their tablet to the ground in the panic. The camera light kept blinking as the small lens continued to capture the moment. The chamber whirred to life and began pumping excessive energy into the outpost. An unholy wailing reverberated through the corpse as London pulled the oven door open.

Tripping over their own feet, they tumbled to the ground and nearly impaled their scalpel through their jaw in the process. They shoved the sharp object to the side and frantically stood. They pushed the gurney toward the opening and gripped hold of the soil-caked boots. With panic-induced strength, they attempted to shove the body forward as it tried to wail in rebellion.

"I'm sorry!" London cried out in anguish as they forced the watery corpse to the damning pull of the fire.

The heavy body, unable to pry itself from the table, lifted its hand only a few inches from the cold slab. Outstretched with fear, it trembled with weakness. London stopped their attempts. They watched its fingers slowly sign R-A-Y-M-O-N-D before it pointed back to itself, then opened its palm upward. It was a welcoming gesture, one that felt fearful and desperate.

London approached the side of the gurney, watched the unsteady liquified eyes turn their melted parts toward them. They took the stranger's hand. It felt like a medical glove filled with water, but the bones within gripped back.

"I don't know what to do," they said quietly, hardly audible over the sound of the oven powering on.

The weakening corpse patted its pocket. London, fingers trembling, reached inside. They found a folded paper, a picture, and studied the faded image. The man looked happy. The woman at his side was smiling widely, glowing with the expectancy of new life swelling in her stomach. The date scribbled on the back was pre-launch, back on Earth. How long ago that must have been for him. They couldn't fathom a guess.

H-O-M-E the stranger spelled with unsteady fingers. He must not have known the dire state of his body. How could he? He was snatched up by his team, shoved into a box, and left alone in the darkened wall of the lab without a sound to be heard for hours.

London picked up a metal tray that held their tools and angled it so he could look upon himself, look upon what he had become. The deep blue eye shifted to the metallic object and studied the reflection on its dented surface.

"I think... you're dead," London said, unable to believe the words they spoke.

Logic and science held no power here. Not in this moment. They had no words or inkling of how to describe what he was, what had happened, but they knew it was not a plausible occurrence for the rules of life they once knew. Something out here, out in this vast expanse of hellish nothingness, rewove the fabric of reality, and they no longer held the power. They were in a land of unfathomable unknowns that would upend everything, and here, in this place, the dead still moved.

"I'll make sure you get home," London promised, tears streaming down their face as they pocketed the photo.

He happily held their hand for a moment before the energy left the limb and it slid out of their grip. He shakily pointed to the oven, accepting his fate with defeat and understanding.

"Let me get you some morphine," they offered, desperate to find a way to keep this man from feeling the full fires of hell.

As they turned to head to their desk, they heard the gurney shake. They watched the body grab hold of the interior of the oven. He pulled himself inside, sloshing and writhing with grotesque motions. London pleaded for him to stop, but their cries became lost to the sound of his death.

The lab was filled with pain-soaked screams as the heat began to burn away the half-dead researcher. As he slid into the oven, the intensity of the heat hit his flesh, and in an instant, he burst like a womb readying itself for labor. The whole of his form flooded out through the skull, dripping black and red liquid across the oven's interior. The uniform deflated, and in a panic, London shoved the rest of the husk into the chamber before it could spill out onto the floor.

They felt the sharp heat lick their hands, scorching them through their thin protective gear, and the smell of burnt skin radiated out into the lab. The oven door was locked, and the lab fell silent. Shakily, they pulled the photograph back out. Blood from the burns began pooling in the fingertips of their suit as their flesh reacted to the trauma.

London turned their eyes down to the photo and wondered what they'd say, how they'd explain this, how they could deliver the news in a way that would lessen the blow. The realization that the home they promised to return him to didn't exist was a painful one. That the family he wanted to return to may have preceded him in death, and it hurt. Where would he go? Where could that poor soul go from here?

It was too much. They slumped to the ground and sobbed, unable to pull themself from the lab and tend to their wounds. They felt like they needed to stay until the body was burned. This stranger was alone in the universe, mutated beyond recognition to the point his own team could not identify him. Perhaps others succumbing to the same fate were shipped elsewhere or were unable to be retrieved. Perhaps they simply did not want to acknowledge him. Perhaps they simply didn't take the time to care. London did not know.

It didn't matter, he was sent to their morgue to be handled with grace and trust, and they failed him. Doomed him to a painful, fiery end out of panic and fear without the consideration that he could have been saved. They did not know how to heal, how to save. They only knew how to burn and silence. And oh, how they wished for silence.

"I'm sorry... I'm so sorry..."

VIII

"Listen up, people!"

The Gibraltar research team turned to face Captain Davies with expectant expressions. Temple stood near the door of the cockpit with the expanse of the universe and the rocky, dusty surface of their possible planet before him. Matthias, still looking quite ill, was at his right-hand side with his tablet in hand ready to take notes if needed. Despite Temple's urges to stay in bed and rest, he insisted on being present.

"We've *finally* been cleared to return to our dig site. What the hell they expect us to do there, I have no idea, but at least we'll have boots on the ground. Thank you for your patience. I know the last few days have been a pain in the ass, but you've kept morale up and kept busy, and I appreciate that. Things are going to change around here when it comes to protocol, so make sure you pay attention!" Temple commanded.

His loyal group of researchers shifted to listen to the incoming orders. The team was small compared to many of the others, made up of only twenty-five individuals, and he cared deeply about them all. They, in turn, respected and trusted him. He would always have their full attention whenever that commanding voice came out.

"With the recent incidents on Elysium, I'm implementing new safety protocols. I don't want you all to be scared, simply prepared and aware of possible hazards. Gibraltar is a different beast, but we're still dealing with several unknowns, so let's be safe. Full hazmat suits will be required at all times. Never go anywhere on-site alone, and always keep radio contact open. I know it will slow some of our methods and processes down, but I'd rather it take longer to get the job done if it lowers the risk of losing people.

"If you feel even the *slightest* bit sick on-site, stay suited up and let a med officer know immediately before you re-board the ship. We have a quarantine station set up. If something doesn't feel right, don't be afraid of speaking up. Don't risk the team or yourself. Make sure you use full sanitizing and clean-grab protocols when you collect samples and bring them on board. That's all. We'll be heading down to our drill site to try and make sense of this mess shortly, so make sure you're ready. I'll be in my quarters if anyone has any questions. Dismissed."

The bodies in the vessel shifted to prepare for the coming descent, returning to their consoles and previously halted reports. Many were unsure of what to do with their drill broken. Their attempts at mining for resources to help aid in the progress of their new home planet—wherever it ended up—relied heavily on that machine. Without it, they felt stuck, and could only fathom what their employers wanted of them.

Zeus did not want to waste terraforming efforts on a planet that may not be hospitable, so it felt as if they were simply breaking the place apart to keep idle hands busy and distracted. The Gibraltar team, though antsy and a bit bored, did love the possible planet they found themselves on and did not wish to harm it any further than they had. If it meant spending the days looking busy for the security cameras to keep the damage down, they'd gladly do so. Temple could not have been prouder of his people.

The captain turned to look at Matthias. The admin stared off into the distance with a slow, uneven blink to his blue eyes, and his dry lips were parted with desperation to take a breath that mattered. As he tried to fix his posture, he almost dropped to his knees. Temple snatched him up by the arm and turned his large frame to hide him from view and questioning eyes.

"I need to take you to the med bay. This has gone on too long," Temple stated firmly.

"No," Matthias mumbled.

Temple sighed. "Come on. We need to talk."

Matthias blinked his eyes open and looked up at Temple. The captain could feel him going limp, so he snatched him up and held him close to his chest. Those who remained in the cockpit looked on with worry. Despite their captain's attempts at hiding his failing health, the crew could see the beloved admin was growing sicker by the hour. The tablet in his hands hit the floor as he fully succumbed to his illness and lost consciousness in the captain's arms.

Temple hurried down the corridor. He could feel Matthias' sweat-soaked uniform clinging to his body. As he made for the med bay, he stopped and turned the corner despite the ill feelings that swelled in his chest. Something had spooked the young man, and though he desperately wanted to get him relief, he knew he couldn't betray his trust by taking him to a place that instilled fear. Matthias was smart. He had his reasons to be cautious, and Temple needed to believe him.

"Captain," Matthias whimpered.

"I've got you; you're alright," Temple assured as he pressed his hip into the security scanner. It read the ID card in his pocket and allowed him entry.

The room was chilled, and the evidence of cohabitation lingered. A makeshift bed was set up, and Matthias had hardly moved from it other than to empty his stomach. Many half-drunk water bottles were scattered about the floor, and the thin metal waste bin that he clung to while sleeping had begun to bend. Temple was growing worried, and his efforts to reach London had been unsuccessful, making his ability to clearly theorize about what may be ailing his aide diminish significantly. He needed their understanding of anatomy, but they withdrew too heavily and refused contact. It both angered and frightened him that they were so caught up in their frustrations that they refused to acknowledge the messages when their dearest student was in need of their help. He only hoped they had turned off their devices and weren't in danger.

Gingerly, he set Matthias down in his office chair and placed his fingers against his neck. The human body was not his specialty, but he at least knew how to check his heart rate enough to see that the poor organ was racing.

"Why are you refusing medical care?" Temple asked sternly.

"I don't want to die, Cap," Matthias replied.

"Explain."

Matthias coughed and tried to fix his posture. Temple popped open his small fridge and grabbed a chilled water bottle. He handed it to the younger man and urged him to drink. He could smell the fruity aroma of high glucose coming from his tongue and felt the sallowness of his skin against his fingertips.

"There's an unauthorized chat board... for the admins, so we can keep track of the projects, and each other. I don't post because I don't trust Zeus and I don't trust anyone out here. I don't want to jeopardize the team if it gets discovered. But I see things. A..." He stopped and sipped the water. "...new board came up about a month ago, noting a stomach virus rolling through some of the research teams. Not an alarming amount but enough to cause a few red flags to pop up. Not everyone was getting sick, but they get sick with the same symptoms I have... the exact same... damn... symptoms. Five of the people who were sick went to their med bays..."

"Drink your water, take a breath, and tell me what happened."

Matthias took another drink and let his tired, emptied lungs fill before he collected his thoughts and finally admitted his fears.

"All of them wound up dead within hours of being seen. I don't... want to die... because of them, Temple," he explained.

"Are you positive?"

"They were all on the Elysium team. Something is happening there—"

"And you're *here*—"

"The guy I hooked up with on leave is on their ground team..."

Temple exhaled and set his hands on his hips. His poor admin; he must have been so lonely. This existence was a frightening one, isolated and so far removed from the comforts and warmth of community and companionship. He couldn't chide him for being somewhat irresponsible with his lust, but it did seem out of character for him. He also didn't need any added stress or worry, so the captain kept his opinions to himself.

Temple booted up his console and waited for it to connect. "Drink the water. You need to stay hydrated. Give yourself some insulin, too," he commanded as he logged into his chat program. He pulled up Matthias' continuous glucose monitoring program and let the little machine read his numbers while he waited.

The irritating trill of an attempted connection rang out through the room as Temple headed to the door to ensure it was closed. The screen suddenly became awash with the vibrant colors of a familiar lab, and the confused face of Doctor Elizabeth Fontaine appeared. She exhaled the smoke from her vape out of the side of her mouth. The reflection of a beaker nearly bubbling over could be seen in the lenses of her oversized spectacles, and her shaved head was wrapped up with a silk scarf.

She looked surprised.

"Temple?"

"Liza, I need you to help me with something," Temple requested.

"If it's about the *dust bunny* London processed the other day, I'm looking at the bio-bin as we speak. Hitomi has asked me about it plenty of times. I don't need you hounding me over it, too. We had four more dead bodies arrive this morning, and I've been running so many damn samples my computer's near to crashing."

"Matthias is sick."

Liza cocked an eyebrow up as she chewed on her lip ring. She turned her gaze toward the side and noticed the shivering admin who could hardly keep his eyes open. The scientist leaned in close to the camera, nearly obscuring the view with her deep brown eye and long, spidery eyelashes.

"Don't you have a med bay? I'm not a doctor," she questioned.

"He's suffering from sharp abdominal pains and bad nausea with a high fever, and it's been going on since our leave last week after he met up with a member of *your* ship. He can't hold down food, his heart is racing, he throws up everything he eats, and he's dehydrated. It's destroying his blood sugar levels. He's... he's hitting diabetic coma territory if we don't do something. Does it sound familiar?" Temple asked.

"The flu?"

"Does it sound like any recent *deaths* you've had?"

Liza finally pulled back from the camera and sat in her chair. She seemed to understand. Looking over her shoulder to ensure no one else was in the lab, she crossed her arms and leaned forward a bit. A seriousness overtook her, one that caused Temple to become concerned.

"Has he taken any medication given to him by a Zeus team member? Other than his insulin?" Liza asked.

Matthias nodded and pointed to the container on the captain's desk.

"Yes, he said he got them from the quick-hop care station on *The Olympia* before he left. Small... green pills, but he's thrown up practically everything in his system the last few days. I think he's had a cup of broth since we returned to the ship and that's it. He did try to eat some pulled noodles, but he started vomiting about an hour later. It's been days. He can't keep going like this," Temple explained as he shook the bottle.

"He needs to stop taking the meds."

"Why?"

Liza pushed her glasses up and steeled herself, "I don't have any definitive proof but... I'm noticing a pattern, and I think something... something is going on behind the scenes, especially here on Elysium. I think the project's fucked and they're *handling* it. That's all I can say. I do know that the meds everyone takes when they complain of these stomach issues seems to make it worse. Don't let him drink any water from the ship's system, do not leave him alone with a med officer, and let me know immediately if anyone else starts getting sick.

"What I've seen has been isolated to the Elysium team so far, but I did hear that a researcher from the Arcadia project—that class-1 sphere that collapsed a few months ago—visited the Elysium mining site for a possible transfer, got sick, and died a few days ago, so it may be spreading. And I just got a report that someone from the Shangri-La team recently complained of the same symptoms but died a few hours after she fell ill. Try to keep him quarantined and hydrated with clean water."

"Is it an outbreak of something on the sphere?" Temple questioned, brows furrowed with deep concern.

Liza shook her head, "I think it may be man-made—"

A knock on the door rang out through the speakers. Liza shot a concerned glance at Temple. Without a word spoken, they both knew something dangerous was about to walk through that door.

"Don't send them to London," Temple ordered.

"I'll do my best," Liza promised before she disconnected the call.

Matthias' heavy breathing was noticeable. It sounded painful and strained. Temple squatted down beside him and took his trembling hand.

"You're going to be alright. When did you last take those meds?" Temple questioned.

"A few hours ago," Matthias whispered.

"Alright, you need to throw those up. We're going to figure this out."

"It feels like my insides are writhing..."

"It's the nausea. Stay calm."

Matthias, eyes bloodshot and bleary, looked at his captain. He wanted to trust him, but he didn't know if he could. Everything seemed to be working against him, and he was frightened. He missed London, missed his home and his family, and was desperate for relief. He wasn't sure he could make it through the night.

As Liza disconnected the call, she turned to face the individual who had so rudely interrupted her quiet. It was beginning to feel like she would never get any of her projects done with the constant influx of bodies—both dead and alive—that ended up in her lab. The research aide looked at her with a bit of distress in his eyes as he entered the room. It was, indeed, bad news. It was apparent in the young man's expression. She wasn't ready for it. She wasn't ready to face more of her co-workers dying. The ship seemed too empty lately.

"What?" Liza shot angrily.

"It's bad," the aide stated.

"How bad?"

"Nine. The whole ground team out in the quarry is dead."

Liza groaned angrily. This was getting out of hand. Almost every soul assigned to the Elysium project was deceased. Zeus refused to pull the plug even though the masses knew it was no longer viable. No one would want to live in a place that caused such frightening deaths, and news of the occurrences had started to spread like an epidemic. It felt as if they were actively trying to cull the herd. She knew the illness spreading throughout the vessels was their doing. She just didn't know how to prove it, or how to stop it.

"What should we do, Doctor Fontaine?" the aide inquired.

"Let me see them before we ship them off. If we can save Doctor Davies the trouble of nine bodies, we should," she stated as she stood with a flick of her lab coat. "Try not to let too many people see them. Morale is already bad enough."

"Yes, Doctor."

Liza took a deep drag of the mint-scented tobacco and exhaled it out into the air with exasperation and exhaustion. She looked at her console, at the mess of papers and the framed photo of herself and Hitomi in the botanical gardens on *The Olympia*. She missed her. Their brief meeting during her leave had been too short. The quick lunch wasn't enough, and she worried that she would never see her again once those bodies came through her door. Still, she felt obligated to protect London at all costs. Obligated to do her part in keeping a mess from flooding into the outpost morgue.

A sudden thought traipsed through her mind. A timely one that could shift the course of her research. She called Temple again and waited for him to answer.

"Is everything alright?" Temple asked.

"I forgot to ask, what's the soil like on Gibraltar?" Liza inquired.

Temple furrowed his brow and pondered the question for a moment, "Dry, dusty. I would say it's like sand, made of... silt-sized particles, no bigger than that. It's grainy and seems to be high in iron oxides. Why?"

Liza tapped her sharply filed nails against her console and pondered for a moment. Temple could see the cogs turning behind her large eyes and wondered what caused the inquiry.

"What would you compare it to?" Liza pressed for more information.

"A volcanic area back on Earth or... Mars, I suppose, would be the most comparable thing from the little research we had before we left our galaxy. At least, in the area we're in. We have a small working radius, so much of the sphere hasn't been looked at by our team. I can't say for certain outside of this approved sector," he explained.

"I fucking knew it..."

"What's wrong, Liza?"

"Temple, I think—"

Her good-willed intentions were stunted when the sound of conversation floated up the hall. The heavy grunting of researchers and workers carrying bodies into the lab grew louder with each passing second.

"I'll send you a message. I think we're being played," Liza said with a sharp hiss before she disconnected the call.

Damn it all to hell, she had so much more to say. She wanted to call Hitomi, wanted to talk to London. Things were progressing too quickly.

She logged into her messaging app and sent her lover a short but loving letter, letting her know she cared, that she loved her, and missed her dearly.

She grabbed a mask and slid it on over her face to prepare for the arrival of whatever mess was about to spill out onto her recently polished floor. No matter how much she steeled herself, her constitution could not handle the state of their corpses.

Nine people, nine souls with lives and dreams, utterly destroyed. Skin unhealthy shades of greens and greys, eyes milky and lifeless. How did it happen? How could it have happened so soon after the quarry team's departure? They had only left the day prior.

What an utter hell this paradise was. It was no Elysium; it was Tartarus. A brutal place meant only to inflict torture and pain upon those who dared to tread across its surface.

IX

A sharp pain shot through Temple's side, and he woke in agony with a heavy gasp. He could feel the heft of sweat that saturated his shirt and the thin sheet over his body. Scanning the darkness, he found Matthias curled up with half of his frame tucked under the captain's bed. His messy mop of hair poked out from under the edge of the quilt, and it seemed he finally was able to sleep soundly.

Liza seemed to have been somewhat right. After discontinuing the medication given to him by Zeus' medical staff, he stopped complaining of constant pain. He still ached and had a long road of recovery ahead, but he felt less feverish and was able to hold down broths. It left Temple more at ease knowing his admin was on the mend, at least in some small way.

Quietly, Temple slid out of bed and threw on his soil-caked combat boots and heavy winter coat. He stepped out into the hall with haste as to not disturb Matthias and swung around the corner to the kitchen to grab a warm cup of coffee. The ship was quiet other than a few of his researchers conversing around the table about soil samples. He said a quick hello and excused himself.

He needed to be outside, needed to step away from the metal and ground himself to the dirt. The nightmares that plagued him as of late refused to leave him be, and he hoped a few minutes of serenity under the night sky might help.

Stepping out into the bay, he walked toward the short loading ramp and took a seat on the chilled metal. Gibraltar was strange. It was colder than they initially thought it would be and immensely windy. The oxygen levels were low, but the gravitational pull was comparable to Earth. The skies seemed angry, the gnashing of teeth of a planet under attack by humanity. He was informed that a large body of water sat a handful of kilometers away, but his team had not been given clearance to expand their research site. How that information came to be uncovered, he did not know.

He was growing fond of this place, despite its harsh environment, and was happy to have been assigned the location. The universe was so vast in its unknowns, and though the Zeus Project had been active for nearly two years, the colonizing efforts had only just begun. So much time in the early days had been spent setting up outposts, cultivating crops, and assigning teams. Building the structure and framework of the next steps. The true terraforming efforts had only been enacted in the last six months, and the excitement of exploration built up within the colonists to the point that he feared many became too hasty and reckless.

The pain in his side returned. He grabbed his stomach and lay his head against the cold metal wall in a rare moment of visible weakness. Something was wrong, and he couldn't discern whether or not it was caused by stress or an illness. Despite London's disdain for it and his own uncertainty with his health, he pulled a cigarette from his coat pocket and lit it. The warmth against his lips felt intoxicating.

"Can't sleep?"

Temple turned to look up at Hitomi with a smile, "Nightmares," he admitted, more openly than he usually did.

"About London?"

"Always about London. I've been plagued by the memories of the day we were woken from cryo and the sight of them in that bloody pod haunts me. They were so scared, and I was so helpless. I feel helpless."

Temple sipped his coffee and savored the warm, nutty flavor. He looked at his wedding band, dulled and worn from time and minerals crashing against its surface, and felt his longing grow even deeper. He felt like he had fallen into a black hole. He was spiraling.

Hitomi sat on a crate behind him and crossed her legs. She gazed out upon the sparkling sky and took in the deep hues of space. The protective dome above them would occasionally grow darkened as bursts of sand flew over the curvature. Beyond the semi-transparent casing, the rich, warm hues of Gibraltar shifted in the winds.

"Do you ever wonder if the colonizing efforts in our galaxy ever worked?" Hitomi inquired.

"I've been musing about the same thing as of late, actually. We left Earth in such a hellish state, and I know the efforts to terraform Mars and some of the moons had only just begun by the time we all went to sleep. It's hard to say, honestly. I'd like to think that humanity left something beautiful behind back home," Temple said as he sipped his coffee.

"I wonder if we'll find something beautiful here. Something to redeem how horrible our species is... Wouldn't that be nice?"

Temple gestured to the world around him. "I'd say we did, in a small way. It may be harsh and unpolished, but this place is beautiful. I wish we had the clearance to explore it further, but I'm not in any position to ignore orders. I have too many precious people needing me to behave."

Hitomi smiled and gently kicked him in the arm, "How are you feeling? I know Liza hasn't looked at your panels yet, but it can't be easy knowing that something is wrong without knowing what the issue is."

"I'm fine. I mean that. I'm stressed and a bit worn down, but the aches and exhaustion aren't enough to be concerning. I am almost fifty, I spent a long time in cryo-sleep, and I miss my lover. Things would probably be easier if London would pick up the damn phone, but they did read some of the messages, so at least I know they're alive. I do wish they'd at least ask about Matthias. I feel bad for the kid that they're ignoring him, but he's too tired to really care, and we're doing what we can to keep him safe."

Temple finished his coffee and set the dented mug down. He rolled his shoulders to try and loosen the tension and took a deep, slow breath. His eyes moved to the universe above him and studied the stars. He wondered where his lover was among the sparkling mess.

Zeus' ships were mostly windowless, so he never knew where he was once he left the safety of Gibraltar's soil. He was thankful they were at least close, within a few hours, so when last-minute leave was granted, he was able to make haste back home to their arms. He hated the secrecy of his employers, but he refused to dwell on it since it was out of his control. The less brain power he spent on it, the less he'd worry and fret. He couldn't risk jeopardizing London's safety by delving into matters that he did not have the power to reconcile on his own.

He wondered what London would look like here, standing still against the dusty horizon line, lit up with red and orange hues in the glow of real, natural light. The pangs of guilt for what his actions did to his lover returned. They could have spent the last of their days at home, sitting on their porch looking out over their small garden in the chill of autumn as they turned grey and wrinkled together.

He yearned for that simplicity, yearned for the broken promise that he would never let his arms leave their waist, that they would always be warm in the sunlight, and he would hold them every night as they slept. He'd have found a way to be alright hanging up his gear and staying home if he only knew what his urgent yearnings would do to their lives.

The regrets grew like invasive weeds in his mind, and he wished he were home. He took a deep drag and exhaled the minty tobacco smoke as he let his mind go back to the dark places it kept slipping into. The ways he could mutilate his arm, blind himself, or paralyze his body kept rolling through like a slideshow presentation. All done in desperation, all conjured in a frantic need to go home to London that kept building upon itself.

"I'm a horrible husband," Temple admitted.

"Well... I wouldn't say horrible. You have issues, but you desperately love your partner, and no one can dispute that fact," Hitomi replied.

"I am, though. I wasn't there for them when they miscarried, I practically missed Hunter's birth, and I wasn't there when he died. I wasn't home when London's mother passed, and I haven't been there for them through any of this mess. All because of my damn job, because of my idiotic need to be *something*," he said, the obvious guilt was heavy in his voice.

"Temple..."

As the captain went to refute any kind words his friend would offer, his thoughts were interrupted by the arrival of a small, sleek, black ship bursting through the dusty skies. He dropped his dying cigarette in the earthy-smelling coffee remnants and stood as the drop ship docked outside of the dome. The air outside was thin, hardly breathable, but it was enough to allow the monster de-boarding the ship to walk out onto the dusty surface without much issue.

Hitomi grimaced.

"I'm going to give that bitch a piece of my mind," she grumbled.

"No," Temple said with a raised hand. "You're going to go and stay with Matthias to make sure he's not seen by anyone."

"Temple—"

"Please. He's the priority right now. Don't stir up trouble that we can't compensate for. I need you to trust me. This isn't a fight we need."

Hitomi, eyes locked on the black-clad form of Doctor Nikita Romanov and her two escorts, snarled but relented. She slid off of the crate she was perched upon and walked back into the ship. Temple slid his hands into his coat pockets and made his way toward the dome entrance to intercept his employer before she had the chance to cause trouble.

"You're up early, Captain," Doctor Romanov snickered.

Her short stature did little to betray the intense and commanding presence she held. The sharp points of her uniform shoulders gave her a wicked air, and her razor-sharp, perfectly trimmed black hair hid most of her face. The twist of her lips, amplified by dark lipstick, was vile and showed little empathy or humanity.

"Why are you here, Nikita?" Temple asked curtly.

"Direct and to the point! I love it. Where's the rest of your motley crew?"

"Asleep. Seeing as we've gotten no direction and our drill is broken, we're shit out of luck and biding our time until we can work again."

"You make it sound like it's my fault."

"I'm not in the mood for your bitchy attitude and disgusting attempt at pretending to be human. Either say what you need to say or leave. You've done enough damage to my team, and I'm tired of you interrupting our workflow and lives because you don't know how to properly run an operation."

The faux-friendly demeanor she held vanished. A stark, emotionless visage became plastered over her face for a brief moment before a sadistic grin curled with the prominent lines of her painted lips. She grabbed hold of the collar of his coat and looked up at him.

"I need your outpost code," she demanded.

"Not going to happen," Temple snapped.

"Your idiot of a partner seems to be too unstable to properly handle the tasks we've given. The empty cryo-coffins, lack of returned bodies and completed reports are... concerning, so I need to do an inspection to see why they're fumbling their only fucking job."

Temple's clenched fist tightened to the point it broke skin. She stroked the fur-lined collar of his coat and softly tapped his face, angering him more and more with every motion of her fingers and vile word out of her mouth.

"*You* are overloading them with problematic issues. *You* are fucking up their mental stability. *You* are the idiot who is refusing to pull the plug on dangerous habitats and racking up a body count. That's not on them, it's on your piss-poor leadership. London is fine. They're following your protocol to the letter. You want the bodies back in one piece? Take them to your own fucking morgue on *The Olympia* and handle them yourself."

"So, we agree the outpost is as useless as your partner and we can pull the plug, yes?"

Temple snatched up her arm and clamped down on her wrist. Her hand went rigid from the sudden, intense force against her body. For a split second, she showcased a moment of tangible fear.

"Don't do anything stupid, *Captain*," she threatened.

"Don't make me end your life, *Doctor*."

Doctor Romanov threw her head back and laughed. "You wouldn't dare!"

"It's easy to make people disappear. You know that better than anyone. No one here would say a damn word."

Temple nodded his head back to the ship. Doctor Romanov turned her eyes toward the vessel. Her thick eyebrows furrowed. The whole of the Gibraltar team, even the sickly Matthias, stood in the bay. Hitomi lifted a middle finger to address her, a satisfied grin on her face. Every person on the project heard the threat, and all of them were angered by the blatant attacks on London's character. It was apparent that they would follow Temple's orders and the doctor's body would never be found if he deemed it necessary. She would not win this fight, not here.

"Tell Doctor Davies to do better," she said with a snarl. "And let go of me."

Temple wanted to crush her, wanted to bust her head in on the rocky ground, but he knew it would only incite more punishment. He couldn't just let her leave, however. Not after this. He did in fact let her go, but he did so with such force she was thrown to the ground, landing hard enough on her wrist that an audible break could be heard.

Wordlessly, he watched her assistants help pull her from the dusty ground. He could see the rage bubbling over in her as she clutched her hand. All he did in response was lift his phone from his pocket and showcase that he had been recording the entire conversation, proving to her that he would not stand for this level of disrespect for his lover, nor would he welcome her presence at his dig site again. The crew stood with aggressive posture, a sign of solidarity with their captain.

This research team was not like the others. It did not bend and submit easily, and it angered her. She hated feeling this powerless. It was not something she was accustomed to, and it infuriated her. She hated him, hated this damn possible planet and the fact it yielded so much greatness. Temple Davies needed handling so that someone more moldable could be put in charge.

As she dusted her uniform off, she turned back to look at the rebellious captain. "This isn't over."

"I'm not here to fight you, Doctor. But I will not stand for slander or threats to my team and my loved ones. You came here—to *my* project—armed and ready to fight. This is on you, not me. Don't incite war on my planet lightly," Temple threatened as he turned to head back to his ship. He stopped and looked over his shoulder. "And get my fucking drill fixed."

X

Keeping food down became almost impossible. London could hardly stomach tea, let alone a full meal. The chalky textures of their medication felt like rocks scraping against the roof of their mouth, and they could sense a dehydration headache settling into their frontal lobe with a vengeance. They were haunted by the occurrence in the lab a few days prior, haunted by the faces that looked at them from the faded photo set atop their desk.

Washed in the mulberry-hued glow of their office, they sat in the quiet and contemplated, waiting impatiently as another round of panels spun aggressively in their reader. Temple still had not relented in his attempts at contacting them. Though they lessened, the regular check-ins left them at peace knowing he was still alive and well. They did finally open some of his messages, so at least he would rest easy knowing they were at least alive.

They eagerly awaited news from the bigger labs about the anomalies found in the miner's body and clothing, wondering what strange new things would be discovered and what odd new death would arrive on their doorstep in the coming days.

A short, irritated note from Liza about a delay in results left them a bit concerned. It was a warning, a dire one, and they could only theorize what it meant.

They were, above all else, exhausted. The sounds in the outpost seemed louder than normal, everything more enhanced and noticeable. They counted down the minutes until the next body arrived. It felt as if the number of corpses below their feet would increase in due time, that the morgue would soon be overflowing with decaying flesh and broken limbs.

Every body box would be full, awaiting their attention. Something was shifting in the universe, and as much as they wanted to warn those in charge of the coming storm, they knew it was pointless. They knew Zeus was behind it. Allowing them the knowledge that they saw the pattern, saw the signs, would only open them—and Temple—up to danger.

The less trouble they stirred up, the less likely they'd be brought into the chaos, so they opted to simply do their job as needed and keep their mouth shut.

They spun their stylus and finally relented to their boredom. Pushing themself back from the desk, they slid their hands into Temple's large black hoodie pocket and decided to hydrate and orient themself. Their motions were halted by a trill from their computer, and it was only when the bloodwork machine finalized their panels that they suddenly had a tangible reason for their lethargy and nausea.

"Oh... fuck... oh, no..." London whispered.

Though it did not surprise them, the positive pregnancy warning threw their universe into a tailspin. The feeling was too familiar, so they had assumed it to be true before they even pricked their skin. An overwhelming flood of emotions rolled over them. Needing to clear their mind, they made for the kitchen to grab some water, stopping to ensure the stairwell door was securely locked as they went.

They wanted to call their husband. Over and over again, they locked and unlocked their phone, contemplating hitting the button and just getting it over with. They wanted to apologize. They wanted to hear his voice, wanted to process this mess, but every damn time they stopped themself. Their mind raced, their heart thumped angrily, rattling their ribcage with its aggressive pounding.

"I need a shower," they mumbled to themself, opting not to let the thought linger and allow some sense of sound to fill the corridor.

Again, they stopped themself. They did need a shower, but the mess from the day Temple left was still splattered upon the tile. The respiratory gear hung from its tubing in the wall, the small pile of vomit that barely missed the toilet had hardened, and their unwashed clothes sat in a heap in the washing machine. They needed to clean, needed to bathe, but they didn't feel like it. They didn't feel like doing anything except sleeping.

It would require an intense scrubbing of the walls and floor, extra layers of protection and more laundry to wash, more time and care than they had to offer. They could use the emergency wash station in the morgue, but they didn't feel like being down there. They didn't feel like doing anything, if they were being honest. Their eyes found the sprigs of basil and cilantro, honed in on the slender stems of green, and reminisced about the amazing foods Temple used to make with the abundance from their small backyard garden.

A wave of confusion rolled over their body as they scanned the long rows of hydroponics. Some of the plants seemed much longer than they remembered. Ivy draped down over the sides of the white containers, strawberries seemed larger, the plant life seemed abundant. Perhaps they had not paid attention like they should have. Perhaps they were too tired. It was hard to theorize. Their mind kept moving to their stomach, to the unexpected growth that lingered there.

Eventually, they re-routed and went for the kitchen again, promising themself a warm tea and a long sleep with the goal of picking themself up tomorrow when their head no longer throbbed and they'd had time to process the news. Perhaps they'd wash their hair in the kitchen sink, wipe the oil from their face and remove their earrings to let them soak in sanitizer. Perhaps.

Empty promises, but it gave them something to hold onto.

The kitchen was chilly. Even with the socks over their feet, the arctic chill of it stung their soles. They snatched up their only clean mug and shoved it under the dispenser. They found a caffeine-free tea blend and let it steep. The floral notes wafted out into the air. Their phone vibrated against their stomach. Their hands nervously palmed the device as it weighed down the pocket.

It could wait. They'd check it come morning.

The warmth of the ceramic was something they savored. Their hands trembled and ached from the burns of the cremation oven. The flesh was pink and tender, and again their thoughts were brought back to the stranger who, quite literally, had exploded in their lab. They couldn't bandage their hands well—most of their medical supplies were in the contaminated bathroom—so they lived with the painful sensation of soft fabric and cold air conditioning tearing at the wounds. It had been a long few days, and their mind needed to shut down for a while.

The mug stung their lips as they sipped their beverage. They decided to finally head to bed. Maybe they would call Temple after all, if only to hear his breathing for a moment. To listen to him ramble about the things that had happened in the time since they parted. To not feel so alone.

As they stepped out into the corridor, one small disturbance in their world caused them to quickly pull their body back into the kitchen. Their breathing accelerated as they rubbed their eyes, praying that their mind was simply deceiving them due to the neglect of their health. They'd left their glasses in their office, so their eyes were strained. Yes, that had to be it.

They knew damn good and well they had locked that stairwell door. Why the fuck was it open?

Slowly, they peered around the corner and studied the hallway. The echoing sounds of footsteps below them twisted up the spiral staircase. They covered their mouth and shut the kitchen door.

In a panic, they ran for the cleaning cabinet at the back of the room and shoved their body inside the cramped, slender box. They fumbled for their phone, dripping tea across the screen as their unsteady hands desperately tried to call Temple.

"Pick up... pick up..."

"London?"

"There's someone in the outpost..."

Silence followed. London pressed their forearm against their mouth and tried to breathe as silently as possible despite the urge to scream. The mug felt hot against their face as it trembled in their hand. They shakily set the tea atop a box of disinfectant wipes.

"I'm heading to my office to get on the cameras. What's going on? Give me some details and take a deep breath," Temple commanded gently.

So many questions ran through his mind, but he could hear that tinge of distress in their quiet words, so he needed to be present for them, be focused for them. London's soft whimper caused him to move quicker.

"I closed the door," London cried.

"Which one?"

"The stairwell door."

"Okay?"

"It's *open*."

London could feel their legs grow weak with anxiety, but the claustrophobic closet didn't allow them room to move. They were utterly trapped.

"Just now?" Temple pressed for more information.

"Yes."

"Did you hear any of the bay door alarms?"

"No."

"I'm logging in now. Where are you? Are you safe?"

"I don't know."

"Shh... breathe. Where are you?"

London heard the loud crash of something toppling over in the outpost. It sounded like metal hitting the floor—something heavy, something angry. The sound was violent enough that Temple could hear it on the other line.

"What was that?" Temple questioned.

"I don't know."

"Do you have a respirator on you?"

"No."

The phone vibrated. Temple was requesting a video call. They shakily answered. The screen washed their tear-soaked face in a pale light. Temple felt his heart shatter. They looked so scared. Their eyes were bloodshot, and he could see they were immensely dehydrated. This was not how he wanted their first conversation after he left to unfold. He saw the cleaning supplies around them and realized where they were.

"Help..."

"I'm connecting now. I'm here. I'm right here, London," he soothed.

"I *know* I closed the door," London sobbed. "I'm not crazy."

"I believe you, I do... and... I see it," Temple studied the screen for a moment, a look of contemplation on his face that was unreadable.

"The hall camera clicked on when you left your office. The door is closed, and you locked it. You're right."

London saw Temple's eyes focus on his computer monitor, scrubbing through the last few minutes of footage. When his brows furrowed, they knew he saw something problematic.

"Temp…"

"I'm checking the door history and lower-level cameras right now. Deep breaths. How are your lungs? How are you?" Temple asked, tone calm and collected.

London wiped the tears from their eyes. How could they tell him they were spiraling? That the voices were growing louder and the guilt swelled so much they could hardly breathe.

Temple saw the damage to their hand, the untreated burn wounds and peeling flesh. What the hell had happened since he left?

"I don't see anyone in the outpost… The gurney with Liza's mushroom project is tipped over, but I don't see anything out of the ordinary. It looks like it's still sealed in the safety case, but I wouldn't go and check without safety gear. The morgue lights are all off, same with the lab. None of the motion trackers picked up anything except for you leaving your office and going into the kitchen in the last… three hours," Temple said calmly.

"The door…"

"I think there's a ghost in the machine, love."

"That's not funny, Temp."

"No," Temple smiled, "I mean a literal ghost in the machine. I think the door locks are malfunctioning. I went back and checked the dates you said you heard something prior to my return, and the bay doors down in the morgue did open and close on their own. I was going to manually reset the system, but I wanted to wait until I heard from you so I could pick a code you'd want. Everything is fine. You're fine.

I would imagine... *Guy* fell over because of the excess weight of the fungal growth. It was moving to one side, so it may have become top heavy. I'm glad you called, though, glad I could check for you. I'll keep the cameras up so I can catch something if anything changes."

London broke down crying. Temple's expression softened, and his heart shattered. His poor lover. He didn't know how to tell them that he didn't have a plausible explanation for the odd occurrences in their outpost. He didn't know how to relay that watching the stairwell door open with no one around, with no one to input the code, caused his own anxiety to spike and his concern for their safety to rise. They didn't need to know that. Not now.

"I killed him, Temple. I killed him, and he's haunting me," London cried.

"Who, love?" Temple asked, confusion falling over his features.

"I can't do this anymore... I can't."

"London—"

They disconnected the call, dropping their phone to the metal flooring of the closet. Curling up inside of the small, cramped space, they wept. Their device kept trilling, Temple desperately tried to reconnect, to check on their wellbeing, but they hadn't the strength or mental fortitude to respond. As they sat in the chilly box, they finally hit their limit and fell asleep, unable to pull themself free of the small prison of their own making.

All Temple could do from his space among the stars, so far away from them, was keep his eyes glued to the kitchen security camera and watch over them. He opened up another screen and scrolled back through the footage, searching for clues as to what happened since his departure. For signs of what scorched their beautiful arms and answers as to what unraveled during their last autopsy.

When the results from the processing came through heavily redacted, mere hours after he last spoke to Liza—who had also gone radio silent on him—he knew something disastrous had occurred in the outpost. Something was coming, and he didn't know how to prepare for it. He simply knew he needed to get home to intercept it.

"Temple?"

The captain didn't turn to address her, "Yes?"

"What are we doing here?" Hitomi asked.

Temple pointed to the bundle on the floor. Under the heavy duvet, Matthias slept, shivering and horridly pale. The stress of Doctor Romanov's visit and her threats against London had caused a panic attack and amped up his symptoms. Every bottle of water Temple once had in his fridge had been downed. Thankfully, the young man had stopped emptying his stomach, and his fever seemed to be lessening, but he was weak and needed rest. The complaints of severe, stabbing pain did not relent. No matter how many painkillers he downed, it persisted.

The captain hardly left his quarters. His team was busy trying to research the massive unknown vein of seemingly unbreakable rock that ran beneath the planet's surface, desperately hoping that it could lead to more understanding and resources to use in their progress. Perhaps, even more so, hoping it could pass the time.

The Elysium project had gone fully dark. No one could be contacted. Zeus refused to comment on the situation, refused to provide answers, and the whole of the Project was in the dark about the fate of the possible planet. Temple found himself concocting a plan, a selfish one, and he only hesitated because it could harm his team's progress and safety in the process. Many dangerous machines and tools were littered about the dig site. It would be easy to harm himself with one, make it look like an accident while still being damaging enough to send him home.

"No word from Liza?" Temple asked quietly as he continued to look through the footage, ignoring her initial inquiry. No plausible answer could be given, so he simply refused to respond.

"Not yet. Is London alright? I heard them through your receiver before you raced off," Hitomi replied.

"No, the doors keep opening by themselves, and I think something happened with the last autopsy that shook them. They're in the cleaning closet."

"Poor thing."

She entered the room fully and stood beside Temple. She watched him study a section of recording for a long while.

"What is it?" she asked.

"They said they left the office, locked the door, then immediately went into the kitchen, but..." Temple pressed play on the recording. "They didn't move for fifteen minutes. See... they stop in the hall and stand there."

"They might be stressed and dissociating. You know that's common for them when they're anxious. Who knows how that autopsy impacted them. I'd never seen a body process report that blacked out."

"I'm worried they're on the verge of a breakdown. They need some sick leave, they need a break."

Hitomi placed her vape in her mouth and took a drag. She studied the footage of London standing motionless in the corridor, trembling, with wide eyes. She could feel the isolation and fear roll off of them, like a child enduring trauma without a hand to hold them through it. It was only when the stairwell door slid open on its own that she spoke.

"Did it record the autopsy?" she inquired.

"I was about to check. Protocol is to shut it down beforehand so the results remain redacted in case the system gets hacked. London usually disarms them since it was part of the deal that allowed us to have the cameras in the first place and they don't like eyes over their shoulders when they work, even ones from several planets away," he replied quietly as he found the start of the autopsy footage. He was afraid of what he'd see.

The gurney in the morgue falling over on its own concerned him. It was a heavy case with a heavy body covered in sprawling fungal growth. It would not be easy to topple, no matter how many lies he concocted to help London believe it was feasible. The morgue was too damn dark. The mess was half-obscured by the middle column of refrigeration trays. It only started to record mid-fall when the camera caught up to the motion.

As much as he studied it, watched the live camera feed and tried to find a reason, the darkened morgue was empty. It didn't make sense.

Hitomi pulled up a folding chair and sat beside her friend. In the darkness of the captain's quarters, they studied the screen as the image of the lab came into focus at the time of their last autopsy. The hall light outside of the sterile environment was off, a precautionary move on London's part to blur part of the camera's field of vision. London knew this body would be problematic; the camera would not have remained active otherwise.

They watched as London, fully dressed in protective gear, wheeled in a deflated-looking body. Temple felt his stomach churn. Hitomi only leaned in closer to watch the events unfold.

For a moment, all they saw was normal protocol playing out as expected. London seemed confused as they narrated into their device, looking at the odd corpse with a stern expression. Temple took note of Silas shifting in its habitat. The captain had never seen the creature move like that. It was enough of a noticeable motion for London to address it, which only heightened his concern.

"Why is it that color? Human bodies are *not* that color," Hitomi asked.

"I don't know," Temple replied lowly.

"It looks like a corpse that's been in water for a while, you know? Like how they did it in the movies? All green and bloated and slimy. Where did it come from?"

"Somewhere on Elysium."

"What the fuck is happening over there?"

Temple only shrugged. He didn't know how to respond. He was too enamored with his lover's motions from the past. Their process seemed strange. He couldn't tell if they were simply being cautious or if something struck a nerve.

The sudden jerking of their frame caused him to stiffen. Nothing appeared odd. The body seemed still and immobile, but London became erratic. The short stretch of footage highlighted a sudden, sharp shift in their movements. He flinched as they nearly fell on their scalpel. He couldn't understand why they were speaking. He wished the cameras recorded audio.

His eyes shifted to the live feed. London had not left the cleaning closet, and the morgue remained without another motion trigger. Watching as the past image of his lover pulled a photo from the corpse's pocket as they held its hand, a sense of distress and curiosity washed over him. A blip in the camera feed turned the screen black. It was only for a brief, split second, but a lapse of time broke the footage. When the screen came back to life, London was scrambling to shove the body in the cremation oven.

Hitomi, sitting back against the chair, turned her eyes to Temple. "They acted as if the corpse could hear them."

"Maybe it could," Temple said sadly, remembering London's cries of distress.

Maybe they *had* killed someone.

"Pardon?"

As Temple turned to respond, a distress signal chimed out through the vessel. His console lights turned red, and the screens were overtaken by flashes of warning symbols. He shot up and quickly raced to the door. The panel snapped open, and he tumbled into the corridor that was flooded with shrill screams. The captain felt his blood boil, his heart race, and his legs move before he could find the will to stop them.

"What the fuck happened?!"

XI

Temple stepped out of the corridor into the bay. The entry point for their ship was covered with the debris of Gibraltar's dusty ground as the heavy footfalls of his crew shifted the terrain. The dry air stung his eyes. The smell of hot metal permeated the area. He turned his gaze up to the safety dome draped over their mining site to check for cracks before he scanned the nearby tenting structures for his team. He noticed a handful of his researchers standing near a crumpled-up form on the bay floor and quickly ascertained that someone was hurt.

"What happened?" Temple barked.

As he approached, he was intercepted by the strong hand of one of his diggers, a brute named Cyrus. The large, intimidating man towered over Temple by at least half a foot, and the stern look in his eyes was a dire warning. His employee merely shook his head, but his expression was unreadable.

"Don't compromise yourself," Cyrus stated calmly.

"What happened?!" Temple asked again.

"Stay back, Captain!" someone else yelled.

Temple could see the panic growing in his subordinates. Despite their efforts to stop him, the captain persisted and pushed forward. One of his younger researchers was sprawled out, trembling on the ground. Her pained cries echoed into the bay.

"Elaina," Temple said gently, "Are you alright?"

The young woman looked at him, eyes wide and teeth gritted. She clutched her abdomen tightly and groaned out in pain. Temple could see her stomach shift and bulge beneath her tight shirt. Her hazmat suit hung limp around her waist, and the stench of heavy body odor and sweat left a fetid aura in the bay.

"Has anyone contacted the med team?" Temple asked.

As he knelt down to get a better look, Cyrus once again stopped him.

"Let go!" Temple demanded.

"Captain, don't—"

Elaina screamed in agony. Her mouth twisted and contorted into a fearful shape, stretching far beyond what could be deemed as natural. Her sternum expanded, and the sound of her ribs cracking signaled like gunfire. Her back arched until the whole of her body followed, the shape so rigid and tense her legs were nearly locked at full extension.

The onlookers shifted back. The young woman began retching as an unidentified object pushed its way up through her body until it reached her throat. Her slender neck bulged as the yet unidentified blockage cut off the oxygen, choking her with a relentless pressure. The flesh began to bulge until it broke, her eyes bugged out of her skull and drool ran down her chin.

Before anyone could truly react or grasp the situation, a black snake-like anomaly broke out of her mouth, sending teeth flying from the pressure of the brute force. Screams of terror broke out as the Gibraltar team scrambled to get away. Temple, instincts kicking in, protected his face as he tried to evade the blinding-fast creature.

It struck.

Sharp spiraled rings of teeth clamped down onto Temple's arm. He screamed as Cyrus tried to grab hold of the saliva and bodily fluid-covered living tube. It writhed angrily as the chorus of panicked shouts and the unmistakable sound of Elaina's body hitting the floor as she died overwhelmed the area.

"Captain!" Matthias wailed from the corridor.

Hitomi pulled the young admin back and bundled him up in her arms. Their concern for the warning sirens pulled them out into the fray after Temple's hasty leave, but this was not what they expected to find.

Cyrus ripped the parasite free of Temple's wrist, sending blood and a blackened, inky substance flying across nearby ration crates. Temple dropped to his knee, clutching his trembling hand with wild, pain-soaked eyes. He could see down to the muscle. The rings of teeth had left hideous imprints across his skin.

Lifting his hand, Temple watched his palm turned from its rich umber tone to a pale, dry-soil color. His skin was drying out, decaying before his very eyes, and the dusty hue rapidly became white and fell away like crumbled chalk in a windstorm. He saw his muscles constrict as the flesh tore, giving way to visible bones in his palms. The harsh force of the ship's aircon caused a wickedly bitter and brutal sensation as it hit his exposed marrow.

"Cut it off... cut it off!" Hitomi screamed in distress.

Temple turned his eyes to her, "Close the fucking door! Someone kill that thing!"

Hitomi pushed Matthias into the corridor then hit the emergency override, locking down the interior of the ship as the medical officers attempted to breach the doorway. The slithering parasite tried to find a new host to clamor into, trailing viscera along with its sporadic movements.

It coiled and lunged, akin to a spring being released from its bonds. Before anyone could react, it latched onto the face of one of the researchers. Their panicked wails as they frantically tried to pull the creature from their face amplified as the sudden onset of decay crept into their pores. Their flesh began to crumble until their tongue was visibly dancing through the window of their jaw. Their eyes popped as they dropped to the ground, unmoving and rotting until skeletal remains littered the ground.

Cyrus snatched up a serrated blade used for opening heavily packaged cargo. Without an ounce of hesitation, he snatched up the captain's arm and laid it atop a metal crate. The finger bones had become visible as the rot settled in and the progression was steadily crawling up his arm. Temple gritted his teeth and shut his eyes.

"Apologies, Captain," Cyrus said calmly as he thrusted the blade downward.

The screams that shot out of Temple's mouth rocked the ship. He couldn't imagine the intensity of the pain that would have hit him had the limb not already started to die. Still, it was enough to cause his knees to buckle, for sweat to crease his brow, and his stomach to violently jump in his abdomen.

The crew desperately tried to scramble away from the writhing mass and pull the deceased body of Elaina from the middle of the floor. No one wanted to risk more of the beasts pushing their way out of her broken frame.

Hitomi scrambled for the handheld welding torch in the corner and turned it on. The blue-white flame flickered to life. She steadied herself as the parasite lunged at her. With a flick of her wrist, she turned up the heat and sent the billowing blue flame rocketing outward. It hit the creature's open mouth, causing it to drop to the floor mid-lunge as fire shot down its cylindrical innards. It squirmed aggressively as the embers burned its body, but Hitomi did not relent. She cranked up the intensity and forced the shaking canister downward. The hissing noise that came from the dying mass sounded demonic.

Temple let out another pained scream as the blade hacked through his arm. With one final, powerful blow, the bone was shattered, and the limb was severed. Someone handed the captain a towel to wrap up his limb. The skeletal hand—small chunks of flesh still clinging to the bones—hit the ground and broke, sending knuckles and phalanges spiraling across the floor.

"Fuck..." Temple groaned.

The white towel became red with blood. He pushed himself up and held his wounded arm to his chest.

"Burn the bodies!" he commanded.

The scared officers looked at him before turning their eyes to the twisted husk of Elaina.

"Now! We don't need any more casualties!" he barked as he pressed his ID card into the door scanner. It popped open and the medical team raced out to try and assess the situation. He barreled by them, heading frantically for his office with Hitomi close behind. She shoved the welding torch into Cyrus' chest and told him to handle the clean-up.

"I will handle the bodies. Get the captain to the med bay," Cyrus assured.

"Keep me posted," Hitomi replied.

She followed Temple into the hallway. He stumbled from the loss of blood but persisted in his forward march toward his quarters, ignoring her calls and urges to get help. He weakly pressed his body into the door scanner and slid into his room as the panel shot open.

"Temple—"

"Put the blade down," Temple said gently.

Hitomi stepped around Temple's imposing frame and gasped. Matthias, pocketknife in hand, stood beside the desk. Tears streamed down his face, and his bloodshot eyes were wide with fear of the unknown. He looked shell-shocked. His shirt was tied up, and a stream of blood flowed down his abdomen onto the floor. The knife in his hands shook, sending droplets of red onto the nearby office chair.

Something moved beneath his flesh, aggravated by the attempted removal and damage. The overworked and damaged nerves forced his body to constrict with agitation from the warring pains within him. Whatever had burrowed into his stomach lining was waking. The sheer look of torment—pure and unyielding—was hard to deny. His innards rippling inside of him, the awareness of the motions of his guts, became too much to simply sit idly by without fixing the issue. He did not want to die. Not like this. Not like them.

"I need to cut it out, Cap," Matthias said, much too calmly for the situation.

He was broken.

"Not like this," Temple soothed. "I'm going to get you... to London."

"It'll be too late," Matthias whimpered.

"It won't be. You're alright. Stay... calm. Trust me. Don't irritate it more. Stay calm."

Matthias' wild eyes softened as he came back to the present moment. The sound of rushed footsteps in pursuit of the wounded captain barreled down the corridors.

"I need you to trust me," Temple repeated. "Put the knife down. Bandage that wound. Don't let them know you're sick."

Matthias set the knife down. He nodded slightly, still unsure and worried but desperate to believe that what he just witnessed would not happen to him. He placed his unsteady palms against the torn flaps of flesh that hung loose on his stomach and made for the private bathroom across the way, desperate to hide the self-inflicted damage from his crew mates.

"Temple, we need to cauterize your arm. Let them help you," Hitomi demanded before she followed the admin.

Temple grimaced and fumbled for the wall to stabilize himself. He slid down the chilled panel and sat on the floor. Blurring, his vision struggled to hone in on anything, so he hung his head and closed his eyes. The ricocheting sounds of boots along metal ceased as his mind switched itself off to numb him from the pain. A soft chuckle escaped his lips.

"I think I'm going into shock."

XII

*W*ake up.

London gasped, their eyes shot open in a panic. The tangible, breathy voice that grumbled into their ear startled them. As their eyes adjusted to the dark room, they remembered where they were, what had just occurred. Their back ached from being slouched and curled up inside of the cleaning closet. The liquid in their discarded mug had turned bitterly cold, and they realized a hefty amount of time must have passed.

For a brief second, they looked at their phone screen and studied the time. Their home screen was a mess of notifications, but the headache that swelled in their frontal lobe caused them to shut the device off and ignore all of them. They had been asleep for hours, it was nearly midnight, and they could feel their bones shriek as they tried to straighten themself up to leave the closet.

Slowly, they pushed the door open and peered into the kitchen. The motion of the closet door tripped the sensors and kicked the overheads on. London squinted from the sudden burst of blue-white light against their irises.

Their legs were asleep, so walking out of the closet without knocking everything over took some time. Prickling points of pain ran across their calves. With strained motions, they approached the sink to wash the sleep from their eyes. They set their hands on the lip of the counter and leaned back into a stretch.

"Now... that's odd," they mused to themself as they looked down the drain of the stainless-steel basin.

A small, spiraling twig of something-or-other had burst up through the food trap. They racked their brain as to what it could be, what they possibly could have disposed of down the pipes to cause a seed to burrow heavily enough that life was able to spring forth. They hadn't the foggiest, nor did they have the mental capacity to formulate a proper theory as to why it happened. Perhaps they'd grab a pair of tweezers and carefully pluck it free to study it later when they woke up properly.

They chalked it up to odd circumstances and the persistence of Mother Nature and made their way to the door. After a moment of hesitation and steeling themself, they hit the command button and watched the door slide into the wall.

They peered around the corner with concern but found themself met with an empty corridor. The stairwell entrance was still open, but nothing seemed amiss other than the rapidly growing plants that, somehow, seemed bigger than they were a few hours prior. With a deep sigh, they returned to the stairwell and closed the door, ensuring it was locked this time by entering the code twice. They felt as if they were losing their damn mind.

"You're too young for Alzheimer's," they promised themself.

Are you?

"It's not a sudden onset of a mental condition, either. You're perfectly sane, perfectly lucid," they continued, hands lifting defensively as they argued with the murmuring voice in the back of their mind.

Remember your mother? She thought the same thing.

"Stop it, stop it... You're fine. You're not going insane, you're just... tired."

London shook the intrusive thoughts from their head. Yes, intrusive thoughts. Not voices. They were not the angry musings and proddings of the bodies that came here to rot. It was their exhaustion conjuring up the wandering thoughts that needed open spaces to roam free. They throttled their mental capacity so often here, it was simply their worn-down lobes and grey matter needing rest and soothing thoughts. No, the voices were not real.

Are you sure?

"Yes," they assured themself.

They needed noise to suffocate these spirits. Needed to clean and pull themself back from this brink and drown their frantic, torrential mind in heavy metal music and lose themself to the repetitive motion of scrubbing the floor clean. To do so, they needed to tackle the bathroom and their own sanitary needs. So, they headed to the messy room and got to work.

Despite the hesitation and delays, London felt better knowing the bathroom was cleaned. They tossed their recently washed, still damp hair up atop their head in a messy bun and finally tended to their burns in a proper manner. Their hands ached and trembled, and it made them wonder what the stranger who exploded in the oven had experienced before that damning pop of his skin collapsed his frame.

For a long while, they stood naked in the foggy bathroom and studied their body. They wondered how long the little life had been forming. The timeline confused them. Before the previous week, Temple's last visit had been four months prior, and they felt as if they should have been showing some if that bout of leave had been the culprit.

Their last panels didn't notify them of it, either, but it felt much too soon for them to feel this nauseous.

They didn't know how to approach it. It was too soon to bring it up to their superiors, and they were prone to miscarriages, but it could be the out Temple needed to come home.

They hid a yawn beneath their bandaged fingers and shivered as they re-entered the main corridor. After they halted the screaming, visceral music that echoed out into the bathroom for the last few hours, the silence seemed all the more prominent. Even the typically soothing warble of the hydroponics did little to quell their still racing mind. They decided to face the basement.

They wouldn't be able to sleep unless they checked. They needed to trust in Temple's promise that no one had entered the outpost, but they also needed to trust their own churning stomach and confirm it for themself.

They went armed. Temple's favorite butcher knife rested in their hand, the metal reflected in the overhead lights with the unsteady trembling of their fingers as the blade bounced in their hold. They grabbed a surgical mask from the airtight storage box on the wall beside the door and slid it over their face as a precaution. If something had managed to crawl up the stairwell, it would have caused a reaction by now, so they didn't feel the need to throw on a full respirator.

It was tiring. Being so wrapped and guarded and bundled up, without the option to choose otherwise, left them feeling empty. They no longer felt human, and they were growing tired of walking around with the delicacy of a piece of paper on the verge of being torn.

The stairwell door opened, and they descended. It was a rare occurrence for them to go to the morgue, but they needed to be sure Liza's delivery was not wandering around. Temple's hesitancy on their call was unnatural. It did not come from a place of concentration, but concern. He was withholding something, and they wouldn't be able to sleep until they could verify they were alone. If it were a person who had caused the disturbance, he would have said something. Something else must have caused the pause in his words.

They stopped on the lab floor and flipped on the lights. The scent of chemicals from the post-mortem clean lingered in the air. Silas skittered around in its habitat, disturbed by the sudden burst of light. London smiled as they approached their desk and set the knife down near their scalpel collection.

"Hi. Sorry to wake you," they apologized.

Silas tapped the glass case with its long front leg. London was tempted to let it out and hold it, to feel some sort of life in their palm, but the risk of it attacking was uncertain. The arachnid was an anomaly, pulled out of the ear of a cadaver in their early days in the outpost. The little parasite was no larger than a quarter at the time and seemed irritated that its warm, waxy hiding place was disturbed. It was an unknown entity—no one knew where it came from—but its massive size upon maturity was unexpected. Still, it seemed Silas was mostly docile and their desperation for connection overshadowed their worries.

They slid a vinyl glove on and popped the top off of the habitat. Slowly, they set their hand into the case. Silas crawled into their palm. It had some heft to its long-legged body. The blue-grey hairs that covered its spherical form were wispy and wiry. It lowered itself down into London's palm and looked upward with its round, bloody-red eyes. Its long legs bounced against their fingers, pressing down upon the digits to test the stability of this strange new perch.

It felt nice to hold the critter in their hand. Silas seemed happy to be out of its enclosure.

They lifted their hand with careful motions in an attempt to not startle it, then stroked its back with their pointer finger. The foreign creature crawled up their arm to explore. London watched closely for a moment, ready to snatch it back up should it get a bit too aggressive. It wandered up their shoulder, across their head, and slid its pointed legs through London's hair like knitting needles weaving thread.

The embalmer sat still and waited, trying to delay the inevitability of heading downstairs by using this as a learning opportunity. When Silas crawled into their hood and pulled its legs up close, similar to the steps it would take when the lights would go out and it would ready itself for sleep, it seemed as if it had little interest in causing harm. The fine, sharp hairs upon its legs stuck to the fabric. It didn't attack. It didn't bite them. It merely sat and observed with wide, disc-like eyes, as if it felt secure by their side.

Feeling a bit more comfortable knowing they were no longer alone, they rolled their shoulders and plucked up the courage to check the morgue. Their odd new traveling companion simply enjoyed the ride.

London walked down the spiral staircase into the lowest level. They took their glove off and tossed it into the hazmat burn bin by the door. The door slid open, and a burst of cold air hit them in the face. Silas reacted by sliding down into the folds of the heavy cotton garment.

Their eyes immediately locked onto the bay door. To their great surprise, it was closed. The camera light started blinking as they entered the frame, showcasing that it had been idle until they stepped into the room. The overhead lights were flipped on and, in the flash of illumination, they honed in on the overturned gurney at the far end of the room. The room smelled sterile. They did not catch a hint of the moldy smell that would linger if the seal on the case was broken.

What if it is, and you just can't see it?

"Stop it, it's fine," London grumbled.

They tightened their grip on the butcher knife and marched forward. The adrenaline from the anger at their spiraling thoughts overshadowed their anxiety. They bypassed the middle row of body trays and headed to the far end of the morgue.

Squatting down beside the case, they peered into the moist, condensation-covered autopsy case. They could hardly see inside with the heavy residue. Spores from burst mushrooms that were damaged in the fall coated the clear casing. The mangled hand of the half-corpse was pressed up against the glass and the slackened jaw was dislocated and forced open by a massive pod of fungi that rooted to the mottled gums. Decay had set in heavily across the body. Its leathered flesh glistened with the dripping water that formed from the heat of the small ecosystem growing inside of the airtight confinement.

Despite the seemingly solid seal across the autopsy table, London could see plant growth running through the drainage grate. They palmed the bottom to ensure the drain was properly closed. Their finger brushed something and felt the obvious sensation of moist roots against their flesh, so they hastily re-sealed the plug and sanitized their hands in the nearby sink.

London couldn't find a good place to grab hold and lift the table back to its upright position. Their hands ached too much from their burns, and their arms were too weak to lift the gurney and weighted case on their own. They didn't want to risk breaking the seal, either, so they decided to let it be. Someone would be by at some point with a new body delivery and they could request help to raise it back to its upright position then.

It was fascinating, if not a bit unnerving, to see a tiny world growing inside of that box. That something as simple as a bit of mold could breathe life into an ecosystem built on the framework of death.

Silas' long, pencil thin leg brushed their cheek as it crawled back up onto their shoulder. It nuzzled its body into their neck, as if it could sense the embalmer's distress and wanted to offer a sense of comfort. They were hit with a wave of nostalgia as they thought of their child-hood cat. They wondered why so many of their thoughts were racing back to adolescence as of late. Perhaps the overwhelming fear and stress had begun to tear at the timeline in their head—a childish impulse to find comforts in parental hands and blissful innocence.

"I should get you some food," London mumbled to themself as they rose to their feet, satisfied that the outpost was empty.

Is it?

"Yes... it is!" they shouted angrily, the sharp and visceral response echoed out into the outpost like gunfire. Silas shifted back a bit from the sudden increase in their tone.

They whipped their head around to confront the mocking voice and felt their heart skip a beat. The bay door was open. The knife fell from their hands and hit the floor with a reverberating clang. Tripping over their own feet, they stumbled as they raced toward the keypad. They quickly input the code and forced the door to shut and lock. The long, dark corridor that rested just beyond the safety of the metal caused their head to spin, but it was empty. No one was in the bay. No one was in the defunct outpost.

It was simply a ghost in the machine. A vengeful, angry ghost made of metal and strings of ones and zeroes. It was real, but it could not harm them. They had to believe the technology could not harm them.

For a brief moment, the only sound in the morgue was the has-tened, panicked breath that pushed through the thick cloth of the surgical mask over their face. Silas, jostled from the sudden forward motion, returned to the safety of the hood that hung limp over Lon-don's shoulders. They brushed back a few strands of their hair that had come loose from the tie and began clapping their palms together gently to try and soothe their spiraling thoughts.

"You're okay... you're okay... you're—"

Someone knocked.

Someone asked for invitation.

Someone stood behind that closed door.

London closed their eyes, clamping them shut as their upper body folded a bit in reaction to the visceral, audible sound of a fist rhythmically tapping against a thick, solid substance. Their knees grew weak, and they could feel the sensation of eyes upon them. They heard something hit one of the body trays behind them, swore the cremation oven handle was jostling. Silas made a hissing noise and shifted, as if to hide from the noises and the body in the case. The creature was hyper-aware of the sudden heightening of emotions in the room.

"You're okay... you're okay..." they sobbed, picking at the wounded skin of their hand as their fingers desperately tried to find something tangible to touch and sense, to ground them to reality as their mental state collapsed.

The voices woven into the morgue's rivets and bolts reverberated with a cataclysmic energy. They no longer remained inside of the embalmer's skull but slithered out through the cracks of the refrigeration trays, through the slit of the bay door, down the curve of the spiral staircase.

Louder.

Pounding.

Angry.

"Stop... please..."

They opened one eye and shifted to look back at the overturned gurney. They saw motion inside of the case. Mushrooms bounced as the body inside clamored to get out. The case rocked and skidded across the ground, dragging the metal table a few inches forward from the force. A loud shot against the glass left a handprint in the condensation.

London screamed and ran for the staircase. Tears raced down their cheeks as they made for the safety of the upper levels. As the morgue door slid closed behind them, they swore a twisted shadow cast by the brutal overhead lights appeared on the staircase in front of them. They refused to look back, refused to acknowledge it, and continued up the staircase.

As they barreled into the main corridor of the top floor, they input their security code and watched as the door sealed.

"Fuck you! Fuck you, fuck you, fuck you!" London shouted shrilly, pounding on the wall with raw anger radiating off of their body.

They saw their warped reflection in the small window set into the door, the wild way their eyes rocked back and forth, scanning the shadows for a phantom that did not exist. They saw Silas' leg poke out from behind their hair, so they carefully extended a finger toward it. A connection to something real. The parasite on their shoulder was real. The shadow in the basement was not. They had to focus on their little companion, on their unborn child, focus on something they could feel against their finger and flesh, something they could feel within them.

Exhaustion settled into their bones. They were desperate for sleep, for relief from this nightmare and the unrelenting noises that plagued their home. With a heavy exhale, they pulled themself away from the stairwell and began making their way toward their bedroom to lie down for a while. They could close the door and shut their eyes for a moment, let Silas wander the bookshelf, and trust the creature would wake them if anything odd happened. It was in tune with the unnatural disturbances on a level that surpassed their own. They had to trust in it; they had nothing else they could trust in here.

They knew that Temple would find nothing on the cameras if they asked him to look, so it did not warrant a call. It would only cause

Matthias more unnecessary stress, so it did not need to be disclosed to him. Hitomi wouldn't acknowledge it. It could not be explained with science, so it would only aggravate her. It was Liza's problem, yet it seemed selfish to bother her with the wandering, overwhelmed thoughts their mind managed to conjure up.

They were alone in the universe. So utterly, horrifyingly alone. Their only companions were an alien parasite that offered more warmth and comfort than any human being could and a fetus they hadn't even given proper thought to. They felt pathetic, but they had to acknowledge the truth through the hazy, foggy mess of their mind.

Perhaps some sleep would help clear their mind. Proper, restful sleep.

It was the only option left for them, and they had to believe that it would be enough.

XIII

The captain, arm trembling with weakness, held up a small glass jar. Its beveled surface caught the irritatingly bright lights, reflecting them back against his tired eyes. He shook it and listened to the jingle of his finger bones dancing inside of the container. His bandaged, wounded arm was wrapped tight to his chest, slung up to keep movement at a minimum and allow the limb to rest. The IV drip taped to his hand tugged as he studied his dismembered appendage.

He hated being so drowsy. The meds that were pumped into his system kept things numb enough to dull the sensation of separation, but he could still feel the ache.

"You should probably sleep," Hitomi reminded as she scrolled through her book.

"I should, yes," Temple mused. "Still no word from Liza?"

"No. Quit reminding me. It's making me anxious."

"Sorry."

Hitomi turned off her tablet, "No word from London?"

"No."

"They must be really mad at you if they didn't respond to an emergency report."

"I'm well aware. It is late, though. Hopefully, they're sleeping. How is the crew?"

"Shaken. They've detoxed the ship, and everyone has been pulled back from the dig site for now, at least until one of our overseer assholes decides to override your commands. Anyone complaining of stomach pains has been quarantined, and anyone with recent contact with a member of the Elysium team has, too. Cyrus is keeping an eye out for anything odd and will let us know immediately if anything is off or anything changes. We did find out that Elaina had been visiting her sister over leave and was complaining of stomach cramps all week."

"And she was part of the Elysium team, wasn't she?"

Hitomi nodded. She took a drag of her vape and shifted her eyes toward Matthias who was curled up in the corner on a loveseat. The self-inflicted pain that ripped through his body rendered him tired, almost more so than the anxiety had. With the stilling of his system, the unknown crawlers in his stomach seemed to sleep. He desperately tried to believe that London could help him, that Temple—once he was able—would take him to the outpost and get him some relief. So, he kept his mind elsewhere and attempted to let his body recover with a bit of much needed sleep.

Furiously, Hitomi rubbed her eyes and tried to keep herself awake. It was a losing battle. She was exhausted and needed rest, but she didn't feel comfortable knowing Temple and Matthias were in such vulnerable spaces. Someone needed to be present and diligent.

"Are you... feeling alright?" Temple inquired.

"Liza and I only grabbed a bite to eat. She had meetings, so our time spent during leave was short. I didn't have time to get down and dirty. I spent the majority of leave in the library and spa. I'm fine," Hitomi assured.

"Good. Hand me my phone, please," Temple requested with a yawn.

The med bay beds on *The Olympia* were less than optimal for a man of his build. The fact that he was so far away from his team, away from the chaos, left him uneasy, but the damage to his arm needed tending to by a proper doctor. He lost the majority of his forearm once they cauterized it. He was glad it wasn't his dominant hand, and even more thankful that someone managed to return his wedding band to him from where it tumbled when his appendage shattered.

"Trying to call them again?" Hitomi asked.

"Yes. I need to let them know that they have to burn any and all bodies that come through the outpost. This is too dangerous," Temple whispered.

"What's your plan, Temp?"

"Protect my lover; protect you two. That's all. The moment we can, we're commandeering a ship and getting to the outpost. We must get Matthias some relief, and we must ensure London is safe."

"I'll be ready to go the moment you say when, Temple. So long as you get some sleep."

"I'm counting on you, Hitomi."

Temple pressed dial on his phone and prayed that London would answer.

How could they? They were too busy preparing for the influx of bodies that had been scheduled for arrival at 0600. Three of them, all from the Elysium team. Yes, they felt their phone vibrate against their hip, but they were too overwhelmed by nerves to re-open that door and allow Temple back in during this trying time. Their short stint of sleep was interrupted by a delivery chime, and they were desperate to return to their bed. Standing in the cold of the morgue so soon after what had just occurred left them nauseous.

The morgue equipment had not been used in nearly five months, so they ran protocols to check that the body coolers were working properly, that their equipment was at the ready, and the oven would heat up as it should. Every other minute they were looking over their shoulder, but the half-body remained still and motionless, the bay door remained shut, and the room was deathly quiet.

They had no plans to start work on the bodies today; they flat out told their supervisor that. Yes, they would assess them, but the morgue would need to be detoxed after the delivery was done. That would take time, they were tired, it was early, and they simply did not care any longer. They wanted to go back to bed and call Temple. He needed to know the truth.

A morbid curiosity also forced them to step back once their initial assessment concluded, to ignore proper protocols and let the decay happen. They wanted to document the changes, the growth, and oddities that would form over the coming hours. Nothing they had seen as of late made sense, so they were intrigued to see what would appear on the fleshy petri dishes that would be arriving shortly.

"Maybe I'll burn the place down," London mused as they popped open one of the cold storage boxes. "That's a novel idea. Set the whole damn place on fire. Use their own hubris as the kindling."

The chilled tray stung their palm as they tested the temperature. It felt good, in a way, especially against the burns and torn skin they peeled off in their panic. The fact that a corpse would soon be lying on it did not cause them distress. At least the technology would be used. It was too expensive and altogether too lovely to be constantly waiting for bodies to hold.

The door chime rang out. London sighed. They approached the comm panel and pressed the button. The small camera screen flickered to life. They were impressed. The fools actually suited up and ran the detox cycle. They could see the green-tinged water dripping off of the body bags. The floor was lined with lumpy forms hidden beneath airtight black tarps.

"Yes?" they asked coolly.

"Doctor Davies, we're here to offload the drop for you. We have followed proper sanitizing protocols," the officer replied.

"The first row of trays are ready for loading. You will have access once I leave the room and unlock the door. Do *not* touch anything other than the refrigeration boxes. Do *not* attempt to open the stairwell, is that understood?"

"Yes."

"Good, the door will open once I'm safely out of harm's way. Feel free to use the spare gurney to offload the corpses... Speaking of, I have a body from one of the research outposts that is in an airtight case, but it tipped over. Would you mind *carefully* setting it upright for me? If I do it by myself, I risk breaking the seal and contaminating the entire morgue."

"Of course. We'll handle it with the utmost care, Doctor Davies."

"Thank you, sincerely."

London turned off the panel, slid their hands into their pockets, and began making their way toward the stairwell. Their eyes turned to the camera in the corner, breathing a sigh of relief once they saw the flicker of the recording light. Usually, they didn't mind these drops. They enjoyed the ability to talk to new people, to not feel alone, but the lingering aura of anticipation for what hid beneath the already decaying flesh just beyond the door stifled their enjoyment of company. It was also late, they were disheveled, and were too tired to play the game appropriately and determine whether or not these individuals were trustworthy.

They ascended the spiraling metal staircase and locked the lab door on their way up. They smiled when they saw Silas curled up atop the rock in its habitat, seemingly resting in the darkness after the exhausting adventure exploring the bedroom and weaving webs in the corner of the bookcase. As they entered the main corridor, their finger halted by the lock pad. Their brows furrowed with contemplation and confusion.

Placing their hands upon their knees, they stooped down to gaze at the small green sprig that poked out from behind the panel. It spiraled on the end, curling up like a cat's tail, and bounced softly in the flow of the air conditioner. They pulled their glasses from their face and studied it for a moment, questioning what it could have rooted to, and how it ended up there in the first place. The one in the sink was odd; a second in a place like this was cause for concern.

Perhaps the ghost in the machine simply came from wayward seeds. Angrily, they let out a tired exhale. They would never get back to sleep after noticing it.

They decided to check on it once they let the drop begin, knowing full well they'd end up removing the whole damn panel in their search for answers, so they made for their office next door. Finally, they pulled their phone from their pocket as they sat down in their oversized chair. After returning to their bedroom a few hours prior and lying down, they fell asleep much too quickly to acknowledge any of the chaos.

Pulling their legs up to their chest, they spun around and woke up their console.

"What the..." London gasped as they looked at their screen.

They hurriedly dialed Temple's number.

"It's about time you called," Hitomi said quietly after two short rings.

"Is he alright? What happened?" London asked as they pulled up the medical report on their main console.

"Something bit him."

"Bit him?"

"Another lovely parasite from Elysium burrowed into one of our researchers and broke out once we started digging again. Seems like the heat and the excess strain on her body woke it up. It killed her in a... quite brutal fashion. The anomaly latched onto Temp's arm; we had to amputate it."

"Fucking hell. Where are you?"

"We're on *The Olympia*. I'm keeping an eye on him and Matthias. They're both asleep... London."

"Yes?"

"Do *not* open any bodies from Elysium. Do you hear me? Do not risk it."

London remotely opened the door for the morgue bay below and allowed the strangers to wander into their home. They turned on the cameras and watched as body bag after body bag was dragged in. They counted five. Not three. What the hell was happening on that planet?

"I just got a drop," London said quietly.

"Be careful."

"I will. Tell Temple to call me when he wakes up, okay? Tell him... I love him."

"I will. We're going to try and bring Matthias to you soon, so don't be scared if someone comes knocking later today."

London noticed her voice grew quiet, as if she were afraid of someone listening. Rightfully so. *The Olympia* was the lion's den, and they were fresh prey to be devoured. They scanned the medical report from their husband's injury. Most of it was redacted, but the clear loss of a limb would be damning for his career.

Their eyes drifted to the cameras. They watched as the two delivery pilots carefully set the overturned gurney upright. The young man was right, they did handle it with the utmost care. London was glad. They appreciated being listened to, appreciated these strangers treating their home and property with kindness and respect.

Another note in their husband's medical file caught their attention.

"Is he alright? Matthias, I mean," London asked gently, almost absentmindedly.

"No. We may need you to... cut out a problematic organ," Hitomi hinted.

"A problematic organ, you say? Would it be something I've seen a lot of recently?"

"I'd say so."

"Shit... Get him to me as soon as possible. Is Temple... okay?"

"He just lost an arm, London."

"I mean... was he alright before that?"

They were met with silence. A concerning line in their husband's file caught their attention. His platelets were a mess, cancerous, and in need of treatment. Their heart thumped angrily in their chest. The dawning realization that they had forgotten to check his panels before he left settled in. They wondered if he saw them and deleted the results, and it left them anxious. Why didn't he say anything? How long had he been ill? How long had he been neglecting himself? Their mind was racing with questions.

"I don't know what you mean, nor do I think it's my place to meddle. Keep your phone on you. I'll have him call you when he wakes up in a few hours. Take care of yourself. He doesn't need any further stress," Hitomi warned.

The call disconnected. London bit their nail and read the file closer. Temple's panels were a mess. He was deficient in iron, his white blood cell count was low, and his glucose levels were off the chart. They couldn't pull their eyes away long enough to keep tabs on the delivery.

They wondered if Temple had eaten, if he was given an IV, how he felt. The panicked thoughts of missed signs when they were together, overshadowed by their own fears and self-centered woes, caused their heart to sink.

Their strong protector—how much pain was he hiding behind that smile?

"Doctor Davies?"

London hastily wiped the tears from their eyes and turned back to the morgue camera, "Yes?"

"We're done. Is there anything else we can do to help you while we're here?"

London pondered for a moment, "Are you heading to *The Olympia*?" they inquired.

"Yes."

"Can you deliver a message to Captain Davies? With discretion? It's... personal."

The two delivery troopers turned to face each other, and their thick hazmat hoods shifted as they conversed.

"He was injured recently, and I can't go see him. I'm trapped here, and I don't know when he'll come home. It would mean a lot," London pressed further, adding a hint of desperation and a soft twinge of sniffling to emphasize the pain of distance in this dire moment.

"We need to leave in ten to make our rendezvous time. We have a hell of a lot more bodies to deliver to *The Olympia*, but we can take a bit of extra time to... ensure protocol is followed, if you catch my drift."

"Thank you."

London grabbed their notepad and tore out a piece of paper. They wrote a quick note, one lined with love and apologies. In the middle of it all, hidden between the affection-soaked lines, they slid in warnings of caution and urgency with unusual phrasing to cause alarm in their husband. Get some medications, get yourself discharged, get your ass back home. They would find a way to survive, with or without Zeus' assistance.

It would only be a matter of time before someone reported the cancer diagnosis to the higher ups. If he left himself in a vulnerable enough state, at the heart of the Project, they could easily dispose of him. If he managed to make it home before then, he'd be safe. They could only hope the troopers flew faster than Zeus' programs ran.

They sealed the letter, stamped it with their official seal, and hurried back down the stairwell. They slid another respirator and a hazmat suit on out of precaution and entered the morgue. The man standing nearby was taller than he appeared through the cameras. The other individual was notating his report in the bay, unwilling to be privy to the possibly damning exchange.

London handed the envelope over and turned their eyes to the gurney with the fungi farm growing atop it. A scowl crested their face as they honed in on the roots that, somehow, had managed to re-open the drain. The thick, black tangles of vines dangled and bounced as the heavy airflow from the vents brushed by.

They sighed. "Thank you, sincerely. For taking this, and for the help with that body."

"Of course. That sucker is pretty heavy, and I'd really hate for that seal to break and spill all of that mold out. Would you like me to help you fix that drain?" the stranger inquired.

"Would you?"

"Of course, shouldn't be too hard. You may not know us, but everyone in the Project knows you. We also know how hard this is for you. If I can do this to help make your day a bit easier, I'll gladly do it."

London felt their cheeks flush. They walked over to the sealed case and began hacking away at the thick roots. The stranger took the contaminated bits of plant life and dropped them in a burn bin while London tried to find a way to plug the hole. They carefully swapped the broken drain cap with the one from the unused slab and added a bit of sealant to keep it secured.

After he sanitized his gloves, the tall man leaned down a bit to address London. His features were obscured by the dark face covering, but his motions did not seem aggressive.

"Burn the body in tray two *immediately*, Doctor Davies," he warned.

London swallowed hard and nodded. They felt safe handing this note over to this man. The tremble in his hand as he took the envelope from them showcased that he, too, felt the fear of Zeus' actions as of late. It would seem the unease was growing.

"Thank you," London said.

"I'll make sure I get this to Captain Davies ASAP. Have a good night, Doctor."

"What's your name?"

The tall man turned to them. Though they could not see it, they could sense the brimming smile beneath his protective layers. He, like so many in the desolate emptiness they called home, must have been desperate for connection. For life. For someone to ask those simple, meaningful questions.

"It's Hunter," he replied.

Tears welled in their eyes. It felt like fate.

He's not your son.

They flinched. Hunter noticed.

Stop being pathetic.

"Is there... someone else here?" Hunter asked.

London gasped. "No..." they cried.

The pilot waved his companion off, asking for some space, before he turned to address the embalmer. He could hear the distress in their voice as clearly as he could hear murmurings elsewhere in the outpost. He swore someone else was in the room, but as he stepped forward to look around the tray, London stopped him. Instinctually, they grabbed hold of his hand. They were trembling.

"I'm not crazy," London whispered.

"No one thinks you're crazy," Hunter assured.

"I know they're not real but... they're so loud. *So* loud. They won't... shut up. I'm not crazy, I swear it."

"You're not crazy. Are you sure no one else is here? Would you like me to look?"

"I have..."

London looked up at him with tears in their eyes. He could see it through the warped plastic covering over their face. See the distress and exhaustion in their eyes and the need for someone to be close, to stay beside them.

"I... um... I have to head back," Hunter said quietly.

London quickly released their hold on his arm. "I'm sorry."

"However, I do have to swing back by this way later today after my next drop, and I... don't have to rush to my next destination, if you'd like company for dinner. I think we could both use some company. That's the nice thing about my job. I've got a lot of free time on my hands... time to pick up *guests* for a dinner date."

London understood what he was offering, what sacrifice and betrayal against Zeus he was willing to make for them. A complete stranger. The gentle, firm way he spoke led them to believe every word he said. They nodded firmly, desperately. Even if he only returned with some correspondence, he would return, and they wouldn't have to spend the day alone. It sowed a seed of hope in their mind.

"Why?" London asked.

Hunter shrugged, "Do I need a reason to offer a hand of friendship to someone who needs it out here in this desolate, cold corner of space?"

"No, I suppose not."

"Then it's a date. You've done so much for us, for this Project, Doctor Davies. And the Project has done nothing for you in return. Someone has to be there for you, especially since they won't let your husband come home."

"How do you—"

"There is no love deeper in this universe than the love Temple Davies has for you."

London smiled. How foolish had they been to lose faith in how much their husband loved them?

"Bring him home for me," London begged.

"Keep your chin up, Doctor Davies. I'll be back soon," he promised.

They held their hands to their chest and tried to keep their composure in front of this stranger who had done them such a kindness when it was not asked of him.

"Godspeed, Hunter."

"Godspeed."

XIV

L
ondon rolled their shoulders and ensured their protective gear was appropriately secured. Setting their tablet on their rolling desk, they input the code to open the second body cooler and let the system process as the safety locks came undone. The tray slid open and a billowing cloud of frosty air flowed out into the morgue, revealing a body bag tucked safely inside.

Beneath the black tarp, they could easily see the individual inside was twisted, contorted, and laying at an odd angle. It must have been a hasty transport. They couldn't remember the last time they had fresh corpses like this.

They carefully unzipped the bag.

"Fuck," they grumbled.

The smell was horrid. The sheen that reflected off the shaved scalp clipped their eyes for a moment before they focused on the familiar face. They recognized the thick mascara, the hooped earrings, the cracked glasses over her face. Her mouth was open wide, locked by a broken jaw, and her dark flesh was busted and bruised. Doctor Elizabeth Fontaine was cold to the touch and covered in welts and wounds. Something had pummeled her head in. Her neck was craned at a sharp bend.

"Oh, Liza..." London whispered.

They opened the bag to her midsection. They quickly realized that her head was nearly facing backwards, as if someone had taken her skull and twisted it until her neck snapped. They saw her hands were clutched tight to her chest. A small chain was woven around her fingers.

Breathing shakily, they composed themself and took a minute to mourn the loss. It had been so long since they had seen her, this was not how they wanted that distance to be closed. Their worry for their husband, for their few loved ones, grew with each passing second.

They tried to pry her fingers open; her rigor mortis-filled grip was tight. Several of her long, sharpened nails had been snapped. Carefully, they attempted to bend and move her digits, but death had settled into her body far too heavily to allow much movement without force. They whispered an apology as they broke one of her fingers to loosen her hold. They discovered a data drive clutched firmly in her grasp, with a necklace gifted to her by Hitomi attached to it.

It was impossible to know if the young man who delivered the corpses truly did want them to burn her body, or if he had seen the object as he secured her for transport and knew it would be a necessity for them to find it. If Elizabeth Fontaine felt the drive was important enough to clutch like a sinner would a cross, so desperately in death, it must have held something damning within its files.

They were unsure if they should turn on the burner. The body seemed still, stable, and free of infection. The obvious cause of death, from their initial first look, was blunt force trauma. It felt wrong, doing it without Hitomi's approval, so they re-zipped the bag and sent the body of their colleague and dear friend back into the deep freeze.

The data drive was cold; they hoped it would still read in their console. They were glad they stayed awake and listened to the warning, despite the exhaustion that overwhelmed their mind and the call of their warm, lonely bed beckoning so loudly.

Their thoughts returned to Temple and how they wished they could be beside him. They dreaded the thought of having to be the one to tell Hitomi this news, but they were glad they could be the one to handle her body with care. At least they could send the necklace back. Whether or not the owner went with it, that important memento would be safe, and they knew Hitomi would appreciate it.

As they headed to the far end of the lower deck, London sighed angrily as their eyes caught sight of the cased corpse down the way, covered in fungus and taking up space. With Liza gone, they didn't know what to do with that monstrosity. It would be impossible to shift it into the oven and burn it, but they didn't want it in their space any longer.

"I could," their eyes turned to the bay door, "shove it in one of those defunct offices... that's an option. Actually... I wonder if I could leave the mutating bodies in the research pods and turn them into terrariums and let them grow without causing damage to myself. Now there's an idea..."

They started to pace. They hadn't been into the defunct outpost before, but they were well aware of the layout and design. Well aware of the low oxygen and security protocols that would seal the rooms. The research possibilities that opened up to them sent a wave of excitement through their body and also gave them an idea of how to keep the outpost afloat once Temple was pulled from duty.

Those things could come later. They needed to look into that data drive first.

They ensured the bay entrance was locked and quickly headed upstairs to make a cup of coffee and dig into the files. They were too anxious to sleep, not until they at least heard from Temple in the morning. It was nearing 0700. He would be awake soon enough despite the pain and pharmaceuticals. He was a tough son of a bitch to keep down even in his weakest moments. They could only hope their message would arrive in time. The distance between their outpost and The Olympia was an unknown amount of time to them.

As much as they wanted to rest, they needed to know he was safe. Then, and only then, could they allow themself to sleep.

After dropping their hazmat gear into the burn bin, they started the detox cycle and locked down the morgue. They detached the necklace from the data drive and slid it into their pocket to ensure it remained safe during the ascent. They were in desperate need of caffeine and a break. It was so tempting, the thought of burning all of the bodies in one fell swoop, but they were curious to know what the others looked like. They wondered what had assaulted Liza. Or what spooked her enough for her to tumble into something.

No. A wound like that, with as many breaks and contusions as she had seemingly suffered, would have been hard to make from a simple fall.

Someone attacked her.

They just didn't know how to prove it.

With as much haste as the old coffee machine could muster, it brewed a light roast as they nervously paced the kitchen. The warm, nutty aroma did little to help stave off the stench of death that permeated their senses for just slightly too long.

Mug in hand, they made for their office and slid the drive into their console. They crossed their legs and studied the files that unfurled before their eyes. They were overwhelmed by the amount of information. The sprawling dates and tiny file icons showcased Liza's dedication to her craft. It felt as if every second of her life had a folder.

After a lengthy amount of searching, a folder labeled 'dust bunny' caught their attention. They quickly ascertained that it contained the reports of the biohazard bin made from the Elysium miner's contaminated articles. Before they could delve into the contents, however, they found detailed reports from Temple's panels in the mess of items—the ones they themself ran—and their curiosity got the better of them. How many others were informed before they were? And why did Liza feel the need to hide it among the reports about the Elysium miner?

"Why didn't you trust me, Temp?" London grumbled angrily.

The frustration they felt throttled their breath for a moment before they decided to let it go. They could chide him over it once he showed his face again. It was a conversation to be had in person, in a moment where they could hold his hand after they nagged him. Where they could apologize for being so selfish.

They went back to the report from the miner's processing, curious to know what Liza found in her research. No one in the whole of the Project could handle environmental mysteries like she could. The Elysium research team was the largest in the fleet, and she mentioned briefly that someone else in her close circle was a parasitologist. Between the two of them, perhaps answers would be found as to what claimed the life of that poor miner.

London sipped their coffee as they scanned through the findings. "*A common sample strain*? What does that mean? Common how?" they questioned.

In the lines of extensively detailed notes, they noticed a statement that seemed off and unprofessional for her level of peculiar precision. '*London had peculiar soil, didn't it*?' It was a code. It was a sign. Something, somewhere in this drive held a vital and, most assuredly, damning piece of intel. They scrolled through the data of the massive drive, looking for documents, images, and videos with the keyword soil in their titles or notes. A hefty and daunting task for someone specializing in the kind of work Liza did, especially when Hitomi passed so much of her Gibraltar research along on top of her own work on Elysium. It appeared to hold the meticulous doctor's entire library of research.

They narrowed down their search, looking for data created in the last few days. That's when they found a video with a title that was so basic it was something only Liza would choose if it were of the utmost importance. She was an obsessively organized and detailed person when it came to her files, with dates notated down to the second and proper scientific terminology. This was important.

London Soil Samples.

"What did you find, Liza?" London whispered as they loaded up the file.

Their video player opened, and they were met with the very much alive face of their friend. The time stamp noted the file was created mere hours prior, meaning she had only been killed in the last half day. Liza looked frantic. Her well-loved scarf was askew on her head and sweat rolled down her jaw.

"London, we never left," Liza said, voice quiet.

The tone was an unfamiliar one to the embalmer. It was confident yet upset about the surety. London could tell she was scared. That was the thing that caused them to tense. Not her frightening proclamation, but how much she believed it.

"We never left home. I think we're still in *our* galaxy. I think—no, I know—that the projects we've been on were the planets and moons still too newly accessible at the time we left for us to have prominent research to compare to. And now that we've collapsed them, we've been forced back to Earth. I think Elysium is Earth and Gibraltar is Mars. I-I... I think Arcadia was Mercury, judging by my research, and Shangri-La is probably a moon. Places we'd have no way of recognizing. For Elysium and Gibraltar, though, the soil samples matched ones in my database. The dust on the miner you embalmed came from the

Joshua Tree area. Zeus lied. The fuckers lied; we're not in deep space!"

London nearly dropped their mug.

Locked in their little outpost, they would have had no way of checking, of questioning the area around them. To Temple, the dusty possible planet he worked on tirelessly could have been a dime a dozen sight out in the untouched depths of space. How would he have known he was on Mars?

How could those who were stationed on Elysium, after countless years of cryo-sleep, know they were walking on their home planet? One so immensely ruined and destroyed from global warming and humanity's greed that it had an unfathomable, undocumented amount of years to change and shift. Especially if they kept them isolated to open expanses, free of ruins and the remnants of civilization. It would be too easy to control those test sites.

With how quickly the projects seemed to collapse and how much of the Project's staff was quickly dying off, those who started to question the locations and put the pieces together would easily wind up dead in a fabricated accident.

It would make sense. It *did* make sense.

They were probably on a moon themself. With how fast Temple could arrive when his few stints of leave did get granted, the outpost could feasibly have been settled on Deimos. The distance was far enough, Deimos' surface was small enough, and their windows could have been placed at just the right angle to hide the planet from sight.

But why? Had something gone wrong? Did they ever plan to actually go into deep space? Were they simply waiting out the end of the world to try and start it anew once the dust settled? The questions kept coming, and they knew they would never get answers. No one who held the truth would ever speak it aloud, and those who raised questions would wind up dead shortly after. London felt those questions, and their thoughts start to spiral with panic.

Liza took a deep breath and lifted her shaking hands as she tried to compose herself. The video glitched a bit before it started to play again, "They keep the research areas too tight, and our vessels don't have windows, but Elysium has a lot of land masses that look too damn familiar from what I've seen during my brief moments in the cockpit. We've only been here a short time, working in isolated pods of land mass, and they've been picked by Zeus so they would know how to avoid landmarks and recognizable areas. I think people have started to catch on. I think that's why so much of my team has died. London. If you get this drive and it's in my hands, the whole damn operation is dead. We're down to near single digits. Elysium is done.

"I was theorizing that Zeus was culling the herd, and I think I'm right, but I don't know how. It would be plausible to believe they're keeping us quiet so as to not cause an uproar. You would know better than I would since you've seen the most bodies since the start of the Project, but the recent string of corpses that have ended up on *The Olympia* had identical symptoms and a mutated, parasitic anomaly as their only connecting factor. We got some files under the radar from the team at *The Olympia* morgue, and it's not good. Everyone who died from this illness has traces of this same parasite, and it's similar to something we had on Earth. My colleague looked into some of the recent deaths, and his research shows what appears to be a highly aggressive, advanced form of *Leucochloridium*. I don't..." Liza trailed off.

London could feel the distress through the screen. They wished they could have held her hand, walked her through this, and been an understanding force for her in this moment. They hoped she had time to tell Hitomi she loved her one last time. Hoped that she died quickly.

"I don't know how. I don't know if Zeus is even involved or this is just the planet fighting back against us. My only guess is that the medication they're giving those who are infected is acting as some sort of reagent, possibly causing a chemical reaction that induces rapid growth, which is why all of them ended up dead after visiting a med bay. Or... maybe the parasites are in the meds. Fuck, London! I don't know! I don't know... I just know that *something* is killing the populace, and it hunts on Elysium. If you get this, burn every damn body—even mine—and..."

Liza brushed her scarf back. She wiped the sweat from her scalp and shook her head. She had no answers. What could she have done that wouldn't compromise everyone she loved, everyone London cared about? What would this knowledge truly change?

"Tell my lady I love her."

A furious knocking at the door caused her to lift her head. London could hear it, could hear the screaming from behind the metal walls from somewhere in the not-so-distant past. Hear the vessel around her shake and rattle with the heft of an incoming massacre of some unknown origin. They swallowed hard as they realized that the very same unknown now rested just below their feet.

"*Leucochloridium... Leucochloridium...* why do I know what that is?" London mumbled.

They searched for the term in the data drive. It only took a brief moment to pull up a document that seemed to be a research paper about the parasite, added only a few days prior. A photo that had been attached to the report struck a nerve, and they immediately remembered what it was. It scared them; that's why they knew what it was. Why it was pushed deep into the recesses of their mind. They had seen it burrow into the fish in their mother's pond many decades ago.

It was a worm. One that killed its hosts and took over their husks, piloting them like zombies with flashing colors in their wretched forms. Drawing in prey with hypnotizing motions that reminded them of fireworks flickering. The fish in their mother's pond lit up in the deep of the night like fireflies. They watched them through their bedroom window, a beautiful and haunting site that burrowed into their brain matter as they wrapped their young mind around the knowledge that those glittering koi were no longer alive.

It was their first brush with death, and it buried itself into their mind just as much as it had those poor fish, and the theory that a human being could suffer the same fate haunted their adolescence until the thought became nothing but a vague nightmare of their childhood.

Their mind returned to last corpse that had arrived in their bay, of how his body still managed to move, respond, and *live* despite the obvious onset of death.

They needed to send the recording to someone, anyone, so this weight would not be only theirs to hold. So others could be aware of the horrendous situations and lies they had been wrapped up in. But they needed to do it safely, to ensure their employers were not privy immediately. That those in contact with members of the Elysium team in recent days were aware of a deadly parasite possibly incubating within them. And, most importantly, in a way that damned, wretched Doctor Romanov could not dispute it.

That's when they remembered the admin board that Matthias mentioned on one of their late-night calls. It would be safe enough—at least for a few moments—and a large number of people would receive it, across various research teams.

Temple needed to come home, *now*.

As they pulled their phone from their pocket to call again, they realized that the rattling and wailing sounds continued despite the recording before them having stopped. Liza stood motionless on the screen before them. The video had ended, but the agony that pierced their ears remained. Their eyes turned to the floor. The screams came from the morgue, and without warning, the lights flickered.

"Fuck."

XV

The security cameras stopped responding, but that was the least of London's worries. The lights above them aggressively snapped on and off. The hydroponics stations spurted and slowed as they attempted to churn water. The grow lights dimmed.

With the ambient sounds of their outpost dulling, they could hear the violent noises below them with heightened clarity. It was aggressive, booming. They quietly set their foot on the floor and moved as slowly as possible to spin their chair without causing any extra noise. With painstaking motions, they exited their office and peered down the corridor. The hallway seemed endless with the lights dimming, casting deep shadows along the white walls. The doors to their bedroom and kitchen began opening and closing on their own.

They crept over to the stairwell and slid their hand up the wall to try and input the lock code for the door again. That's when they felt something brush their hand. A tangle of wayward, spiraling green roots surrounded the panel, like a mess of hair pinned beneath a heavy slab, bursting forth with enough mass to bend the metal. The panel was dead, and they could only pray the locks held against the misfiring technology.

Quietly, they crawled along the floor to the front of the outpost, hoping to reach the main motherboard and hardware wired into the wall near the decontamination chamber. They needed to try and restore power.

"Fuck," they growled, realizing they needed to grab a respirator from the bathroom.

With the systems down, the vents would be wide open, and the circulation of unclean air would be crawling up the shafts to the top floor in a matter of moments. They couldn't believe they were even entertaining the thought that all of those bodies managed to reanimate, break loose, and wreak havoc below them.

But they had seen it, seen the dead come back to life, and knew it was the only reason so much noise could be disrupting their quiet. They had no other choice but to believe it, and believing came with the understanding that those corpses would be infected and contaminate the outpost once they broke out of the refrigeration boxes.

As they crept up to the bathroom, they saw that the tumblers and circuitry were overrun by more greenery. The doorframe was moss covered, and fungal entities crawled along the winding bundles of evergreen with pointed caps and sprawling roots. Strands of an ivy-like plant stretched across the misfiring door, growing with a sentient motion that reminded them of tentacles clamoring for something to cling to. They eventually wound themselves around the panel and pulled with such intensity that it could no longer move. The gears in the door's mechanics ground angrily against the resistance.

This did not feel normal; it felt otherworldly. It felt as if their outpost of metal and rivets was in the process of being terraformed. Yes, the old gods were angry, and they had arrived at London's doorstep with a vengeance.

They slid inside the bathroom and fumbled for one of the respirators stored under the sink, knowing full well the fungi would be lethal to them, especially if that door snapped free and compressed down into the curve of the door frame. It would burst them like pustules, effortlessly.

Securing the respirator over their mouth, they continued their way down the hall to the main panel. They were thankful the outer doors were deadlocked in the event of a power loss or complete grid failure, so at least they wouldn't be sucked out into the vacuum of space. In all honesty, they almost preferred that demise over facing whatever mess was in their morgue. This nightmarish horror that swept into their outpost felt omniscient, oppressive, and hungry.

They stood and popped open the covering of the circuit breaker box. The system was going haywire. It was impossible to narrow down the issue. Wires appeared to be unplugging themselves, power connectors were being interrupted by an unknown blockage, and the silhouettes of plant growth overrunning the overhead lights cast long shadows on the floor. They attempted a system reboot and hoped for the best, breathing gently to not exacerbate their lungs with the fear that rooted in their soul.

"I need to send that video... I need to call Temple... and hide," they mumbled, trying to give themself a task list to focus on, to drown out the cacophonous noises below them and catch their breath in the thinning oxygen.

They watched the outpost system click green, signaling the start of the reset, and decided to make their way back to the office. Nothing else could be done. The reset would either work or the outpost would collapse. They needed to trust in the system, trust that Hunter would return soon, and trust that they would see their husband again, so they returned to their knees and headed down the darkened corridor. They would handle their affairs as quickly as possible and hide in whichever room seemed the most stable. Sweat began to form on their brow, and their elbows stung from pressing against the metal.

Crawling by the stairwell door, they kept close to the wall and slowed their movements. As their hand reached forward, they flinched when they heard the metal stairs on the other side of the wall creak. The door shuddered and hit them in the ribcage as a harsh force suddenly thrust against it. Their teary eyes turned upward to the small window, and they found themself locking gazes with something shrouded in shadows for a brief but damning moment.

The face was split nearly in half, dangling awkwardly like a puppet, and feebly held together by woven threads of roots that tore and ripped the flesh as it gnashed its teeth. Its mouth sat agape, forced open by clamoring, angrily tendrils of wood and thorns that forced themselves up the corpse's throat. The bulged eyes were nothing more than white discs, pushed out of the deeply set sockets. The body was wearing a spacesuit. The helmet's visor was cracked and jagged, and their suit was coated in black, clotted blood.

It saw them.

It raised its fists and pounded aggressively against the door.

London fell back and scooted themself to the far wall, crashing into the lowest row of hydroponics pods hard enough to spill water down their back. The corpse wailed and beat upon the door. The glass window cracked from the heft of the helmet hitting it repeatedly.

"Mur-der-er," it croaked angrily, the sound akin to the wail of an emergency siren building momentum. It was a guttural noise, one that did not come from vocal cords, but from the soul. It was haunting, familiar. It was the sound that echoed into their outpost, from deep in the morgue, and possessed their peace with damning calls.

"I didn't do anything!" London cried, slamming their hands over their ears.

"Pla-net... ki-ller!"

"Stop it!"

"Stop... it!"

The glass shattered. London's eyes shot open, and tears streamed down their cheeks. They couldn't move. They were frozen in fear and lightheaded from the sudden dip in stabilization in the outpost. Their eyes fully honed in on the corpse's as it fumbled for a way to open the door. They felt the surge of emotion, of a millennia of pain bursting through their head with the vicious connection of gazes between them.

They felt as if they were looking upon the face of God. An angry God who wanted recompense for the desecration of his creation. The corpse was piloted by the rage and pain of a broken Earth, left abandoned and rotted by the hands of those meant to protect her. Yes, the old gods were angry, their temples were being desecrated, and Zeus could only watch with glee as one by one the powers fell.

Every root, branch, vine, and blossom in the outpost shuddered angrily from this being's presence. It writhed angrily, and with a huff, its body tensed as if to prepare for an attack. The window fully shattered from the manic, wayward motions of its limbs and head.

"I'm sorry!" London cried as their vision blurred.

The outline of their eyes felt as if they were tearing, as if they were melting in their sockets like the moist corpse they had burned in the fires below. They quickly shifted their hand over their face and broke the connection enough to force themself to their feet, to force themself to move toward their office. They needed to call Temple, call for help, call—

A sharp pain struck their throat. They quickly palmed their neck and found a sharp, thin spike protruding from their flesh. A gasp was stunted, and they felt their tendon tense as an allergic reaction throttled their throat.

They scrambled into their office and hit the door panel. It lit up green and closed with a rapid, unregulated speed. It hit the doorframe and bounced back halfway, then locked in place as the last of its power shut down. The control panel flew off the wall as roots and vines broke through the machinery.

London struggled to breathe. They would never make it to the bathroom in time to purge the foreign substance from their skin and lungs. The spike was lodged deep into their neck. They couldn't find the strength to pull it loose.

Stumbling, out of breath, and hardly able to see, London hit the call button for their husband. With the last of their strength, they sent Liza's recording to the admin board and prayed someone could stop this madness.

The screen flickered to life as Temple accepted the call with a groggy, pharmaceutical-induced haze in his eyes.

"London...? London!"

Temple saw the blood that ran down their neck, the tears that reflected the warm, inviting mulberry-colored lights, and the fear in their expression. He saw the dimmed bulbs, their strained breathing, and the way their hair began to lift from their shoulders as gravity failed in the outpost. The light in the hall flickered aggressively until it went out.

"Help... Temple..." was all London could say before a harsh, retching sound crawled up their throat.

The respirator was filled with blood as they coughed outward, filling the mask so quickly, so violently, that it broke through the seal and ran down their chin. Their icy blue eyes rolled up into their skull and their body collapsed onto the floor, obscuring them from view. A shrill, unholy scream echoed in the background for a moment, then all fell silent.

"London!"

XVI

"Captain..." Matthias mumbled, eyes locked onto the flood of chaotic messages hitting the forums. His unsteady hand shakily tied the laces of his boots as he prepared to leave the hospital suite.

Temple shakily slid his uniform back on, struggling with the buttons until he finally gave up with an angered curse under his breath. Blood trickled down his arm where his IV had been ripped out, and he was unsteady on his feet, but he persisted. He needed to get home.

"Not now, we need to go," Temple demanded quietly.

Neither Hitomi nor Matthias could argue with him. It would be impossible for London to survive an attack like that. The time it would take to return to the outpost would not allow help to arrive with enough haste to save them. They were dead, but Temple was determined to return, and his crew could not argue with him. He needed to go home, and they would help him do it.

As Temple opened the door, he was met with the face of a young man he had not seen before. One with wide eyes and a bit of a shocked expression in his slightly agape mouth.

"Move," Temple barked.

"Captain Davies?" the young man asked.

"Move!"

He extended an envelope with London's stamp visible in the corner for the captain to take. "My name is Hunter. I was sent by Doctor Davies with an urgent letter... and a request to bring you home. Is everything alright?"

Temple blinked slowly as he tried to register the information that had just been relayed to him, "Are you a pilot?"

"Yes," Hunter replied.

"I need you to take me back there, *now*."

The young man studied this familiar stranger's face and blinked his bright blue eyes a handful of times. He nodded firmly with understanding. Something must have happened after he left the outpost. He zipped up his jacket and nodded his head back, urging everyone to leave the suite. It was still early enough in the day that the possibility of slipping out without too much hassle was high. He offered his arm to Temple to help him walk. The captain reluctantly took it.

Hitomi quickly shoved all of the group's belongings into the pack she quickly filled before transport, ensuring the small Gibraltar team's necessities were safely in her grip. She held onto Temple's phone and kept her eyes locked onto the shaky, unsteady view of London's office as the group hurriedly made their way out of the medical ward. The unsettling sounds that warbled out of the speaker concerned her. They were too deep, too guttural to belong to London.

"Why were you at my home?" Temple questioned.

"Delivering bodies; it was a scheduled drop," Hunter replied quietly. "The whole Elysium team is dead, Captain Davies. The research ship was basically abandoned. No one made it out alive. It was a bloodbath."

"No one?" Hitomi asked with a shuddered, panicked inhale.

"No one," he repeated firmly.

"Captain—"

"Not now, Matthias, please!" Temple interrupted.

"Captain, we need to run!" Matthias barked.

Temple looked back at his admin. He was red in the face, covered in sweat and angry. The tablet in his hands was white knuckled with such force it would be easy to believe he could snap it. He saw something, something more damning than what happened on the still active call with London.

"I need you to trust me," Matthias begged.

Temple saw the desperation in his admin's face.

"Run," Temple demanded as he fixed his posture.

Hunter released his hold on the captain and quickly darted down the corridor, leading the way to his transport vessel. The group moved forward, pushing by sleepy nurses and concerned medical staff that exited their rooms and offices after hearing the frantic footsteps. An angry warning alarm began sounding above them, turning the corridor red. All eyes shifted upward with confusion, and Hunter picked up his pace.

The pilot burst out into the main promenade of *The Olympia*, nearly toppling a scientist with a tray of breakable vials in their hands. Several of the glass containers hit the ground and shattered, sending blood samples flying across the polished metal floor.

A few feet away, down the rounded hub of the main deck, the morgue door rattled. Medical staff members wheeling a gurney screamed as the body under the sheet began writhing. Fearful shrieks echoed out of the morgue, and the door flew open and revealed a woman for the briefest of moments before she was ripped back by an unseen force. A spray of blood shot out across the sterile floor from another embalmer's body as he was impaled by a sharpened root-like substance. His frame was thrown out into the main deck with such force his neck snapped.

Shuddering, slinking masses of rotted flesh, covered in layers of mossy, fungal growth shifted into view. Eyes milky and lifeless, glowing with intensity as ribbons of color ran across the surfaces of their irises, the horde of sentient cadavers broke through the autopsy lab like a flood collapsing a dam. All of them screamed out in pain, damning the onlookers with claims of debauchery and desecration of their home in harsh, guttural voices.

The Olympia was thrust into chaos. Researchers and security guards were mutilated, skewered by sharpened vines, and torn apart by aggressive, violent hands. Limbs were thrown across the promenade. The metallic smell of blood rushed into the hub as the flood of plasma rolled over the floors.

Temple shifted trajectory toward the drop ship dock. Out of the corner of his vision, he saw the stone-faced Doctor Romanov exit her office on the deck above. Her sharpened nails grabbed onto the railing, and she leaned over and gazed upon the chaos with a sick grin emphasized by the black color of her lipstick. Damn that woman; she knew this would happen. She knew this was coming, and she sent it to his lover's doorstep without a shred of remorse or empathy.

It felt final. They needed to hurry.

The growing crowd that scrambled out of the docks caused a blockage in the corridor. The confused and worried populace flooded into the main deck to await briefing for the sudden warning—unable to fathom the hell they were marching into.

Temple pushed by, breathing heavily as he fought against the wear on his body as he followed the curved corridor along the starboard side of the massive vessel. He felt someone grab his arm and pull him down the docks. He was met with the determined eyes of the young stranger who had delivered his lover's letter, locked onto a ship at the far end of the port.

"Thank you," Temple said wearily.

"Stick close," Hunter commanded.

He waved down Hitomi and Matthias, urging them to hurry before the dock was deadlocked in the panic. The angered shouts of guards attempting to halt all movement in *The Olympia* became targeted on the fleeing group as they realized their intentions.

Temple's faithful team snatched up a few spacesuits hanging in the travel-gear storage closet on their way. Matthias nearly dropped his tablet as his body jerked angrily from the excess of stress that stirred up the invasive entity in his gut. It was angry, feeding off of his own aggressive, amplified energies. The group funneled into a drop ship. They tossed the heavy garments and helmets onto the floor as they prepared for launch.

Hunter slammed his hand on the door button and closed up the vessel, then raced to the cockpit. His seat was still warm. The engine easily turned over, and the control grid burst to life without hesitation.

"Get strapped in, we need to go!" he shouted.

With a heavy exhale, Temple collapsed into one of the seats. He clutched his arm tight and tried to catch his breath. He shakily pulled the sealed letter with his lover's stamp on the corner from his pocket. Hitomi approached. She carefully buttoned Temple's uniform top for him and slid the safety belt over his lap, knowing full well his mind was elsewhere.

"Are you alright?" he asked gently.

"No," she replied, voice quiet and shaky. "Want me to open that? Your hand is trembling."

"Would you mind? I'm having a hard time."

She swapped out the letter for his phone. He held the device up and looked at the image of his lover's office. Occasionally, he'd see the flicker of lights through the crack in the door, so he knew the feed was still active. He saw the leaves of the plants under the grow lights move, but he was unable to tell if it was caused by the unstable gravity levels or the air circulation from the vents.

The noticeable increase in growth was now slightly obscured in the low lights, but he saw vines and buds in places they should not have been, too large compared to when he last saw them in person to be logically feasible. He felt as if he were gazing upon an abandoned building back on Earth, reclaimed by Mother Nature after years without humanity's interference rotting it to the core. That much growth in such a short amount of time was impossible.

Hitomi tore open the envelope and pulled the letter out for him to easily grab.

"Captain?" Matthias said with a heavy pant.

He groaned out in pain and clutched his stomach as the drop ship shot out of the dock and into the vastness of space. Temple went to stand and go to his aid but was stopped by Hitomi's calm hand on his chest. She handed the letter back to him and went to the admin's side. Gently, she wiped the tears from Matthias' bloodshot eyes and helped him into one of the seats.

"What's going on, Matthias?" Temple asked as he set his phone on a nearby shelf.

He felt guilty for snapping at him and wanted to give Matthias the full of his attention while he could. It was obvious the young man was scared, that something had happened that rattled him to the core.

"A... video hit the admin board. It's Doctor Fontaine... it looks like it may have to do with what just happened..." Matthias trailed off, shakily handing over his tablet to Hitomi.

He set his hand on his stomach and laid his head back. Adjusting to the sudden shift in gravity and speed caused his innards to shriek, so he maneuvered his body a small bit at a time until he found a comfortable place to lean with his legs draped over the arm of the uncomfortable flight seat.

"Have you watched it?" Temple inquired.

"No, it hit the board right as Doctor Davies called, but it can't... be a coincidence," Matthias replied with a heavy exhale. "What does the letter say?"

Temple opened the letter and looked at the contents. He felt his heart thump angrily as he read the panicked scrawling made up of *I love you*s and *come home*s. Something had spooked them. In the middle of it all, they noted something about his star sign, how they always felt they were made for each other, as if the alignment of the planets ordained it long before they were even born. How he was akin to a medicine for them, something desperately needed and more important than breathing. It caused him to pause. His birthday was in April. He wasn't a cancer.

All of the sweet words meant nothing once he found the final sentence. It wasn't the harsh ramifications of the diagnosis they proposed that shook him the most, not in the slightest. It was the mention of a new galaxy blooming at the center of their world that caused his heart to race.

"Temp?" Hitomi questioned.

Temple lifted his gaze to find all three of the individuals in the tight ship staring at him with anticipation.

"A love letter, asking me to come home. Shall we hear what Liza felt important enough to disrupt the whole of the Project over?" Temple offered, breath a bit shaky as he wrestled with the realization of what his lover's letter insinuated. He was dying, and his lover was with child.

Silent, judgmental, and worried glances were shared between the others, but Hitomi finally pressed play on the recording. Doctor Fontaine's frantic voice came through the small speakers. Everyone listened to her hypotheses with intent and curiosity.

Hitomi handed the tablet back to Matthias and began pacing, unable to stomach it when her partner admitted that the only way London would have access to this file would mean her death had arrived. Temple simply listened with quiet contemplation, his own eyes locked onto the video feed of the office where he last saw his lover.

They all felt so foolish, so manipulated and used.

"What do we do? What if this is true?" Matthias proposed.

"I don't know. There will probably be riots and more deaths, but I don't know. Those... things that broke out of the morgue didn't bode well for the populace, either," Temple replied with a slow, pained exhale. His meds were wearing off. He could feel the throbbing of his amputated arm, the crawling of his skin, and the thump of his heart from the anxiety of it all.

"It's strange how plausible it all is, isn't it?" Hunter mused, finally chiming into the conversation.

"More plausible than the literal walking corpses," Hitomi grumbled.

"Was anything off when you did your drop? How did the outpost look? The corpses?" Temple asked of the stranger.

"The outpost and Doctor Davies seemed fine, if not a bit tired and needing some company. A few strange noises popped up. I thought it was another person, but they assured me they were alone. We followed protocol to the letter, detoxed the bay before entry and doubled up the hazmat suits. We did everything the way we should have, even ensured the bodies were on the appropriate trays so they didn't have to struggle to transport them onto gurneys. They were heavy and dead. Nothing... I was going to say nothing was odd, but the bodies were in bad shape. We bagged them too fast for me to really take a look.

"We packed up twenty bodies, Captain. I can't really recall specifics. We were ordered to pick a few at random, so I can't be certain which ones ended up in Doctor Davies' care. I did tell Doctor Davies about the body in tray two, I think it was Doctor Fontaine, so I made certain to mark that body bag and get it to them but…" Hunter looked over his shoulder and held his tongue. "I noticed a drive in the body's hand when I packed them up, so I told them to burn it, hoping it was subtle enough to not raise alarm but worrying enough to make sure they checked it before the chill damaged it."

"Was she bald? With green glasses?" Hitomi inquired.

Hunter nodded slightly. Hitomi bit her lip and placed her hands on her hips, trying to keep her fury in check. A warning light popped up on the dash, signaling a contact channel was requested from *The Olympia*. He turned it off and picked up the pace, hoping to put more distance between their small drop ship and the massive vessel.

"How can we trust you? We don't even know you. How can we trust you're going to take us to the outpost?" Matthias asked with a nervous and angered nature.

"My name is Hunter McCall. My wife helped stabilize Doctor Davies when their cryogenics chamber broke. Doctor Davies did us a kindness recently, one we can never repay them enough for, so I wanted to do what I could for them. They asked me to deliver a letter, so I did. You asked me to get you home, so I will," Hunter assured.

Temple rubbed his eyes. His leg bounced with irritation and worry. How did things fall apart so quickly? How would he cope if he walked into his home with these wounded, scared individuals, only to find his London, his life, his everything, dead in their office? He had to believe they survived. He had to.

As Hitomi parted her lips to speak, she heard a soft sound from somewhere in the ship.

Temple turned his eyes to follow, looking down at his phone with bated breath.

"Temple?"

"London?!"

"It's dark..."

"Hang on, love, we're coming. Hang on."

Hitomi brushed her hair back and looked at Matthias. The admin, tears streaming down his cheeks, sat in disbelief. It was impossible, but he was elated. Even Hunter's shoulders went slack as he released the worried tension he harbored. He was thankful his wife was far off at another research post, away from the mess and chaos. At least, for the moment.

"I think I lost the baby... Temple... It's so dark..."

Temple felt his heart drop into the pit of his stomach and tears well in his eyes. Hunter whipped around in shock. His gaze darted to the people behind him and their mortified expressions as the reality of the doctor's soft cries settled in. Matthias clamped his hands over his mouth to stifle a sob.

Temple sniffled. "I'm sure... everything's fine... I'm coming home, London."

"We'll be there in about an hour. I'll try to be quicker if it's safe enough for me to pick up speed. I'll get you home, Captain," Hunter assured.

Temple set the phone against his lips and prayed for their safety. "I'm coming home... London, I'm coming home. Wait for me."

XVII

"What's the plan, Temple?" Hitomi asked as she slid a slightly ill-fitting spacesuit on.

"I don't have one. I don't know what we're walking into, but it looks like there's been some level of power failure in the outpost, so we need to work to restore it once we're sure London is safe. The issue is... can you help me, please?" Temple trailed off with an exasperated groan.

Hitomi sniffled and smiled a bit. Her nose was red, and her eyes were puffy from crying in Temple's arms. She could allow herself to be vulnerable for a moment, allow herself to mourn the loss before shifting her mindset. Once they touched down, her only goal would be destroying everything Zeus stood for. She wanted to paint their ships red and hang Doctor Romanov's head from the balcony of *The Olympia*.

She helped him slide the ill-fitting space suit on. Temple looked over his shoulder at Matthias who was curled up on the floor. The small space seemed to help calm him, as did the relentlessly cold air inside of the drop ship, and it troubled Temple deeply to wake him.

"Thank you. As I was saying, in the event of any level of power failure, the outer bay doors will remain under strict lock procedures so as to not break the seal and compromise the outpost," Temple explained.

"Which means we won't be able to get in through the front door," Hitomi mused.

"We'll need to go through the defunct outposts and make our way into the morgue. That door isn't connected to an exterior wall, so we should be able to bypass it even if the power levels aren't optimal. It will just take some rebooting, or forceful entry."

"Which means walking through a dark, unfinished lab and straight into an unknown threat. Sounds fun."

"It's dark in there, but it's a pretty straightforward trek, thankfully," Hunter added.

Hitomi secured Temple's suit and handed him back his phone. The old friends looked down at the image. London would speak in small, pained sentences, but it seemed they were dipping in and out of consciousness, most likely due to the unstable oxygen levels with the shuddering of the system and the irritant that crept into their lungs. Temple had no idea how bad the damage was or what caused the violent reaction. Still, they spoke, they were responsive, so the captain held out hope.

"What's that?" Hitomi asked, pointing to an oddity seen through the crack in the door on the phone screen.

"Looks like pollen spores," Temple replied.

"They had a respirator on, correct?"

"Yes, but they're going to need medical help... especially if they miscarried. Hunter, can I ask a favor? I know I've already put too much unnecessary stress on you, but this is important," Temple requested.

"Of course," Hunter assured as he slowed the ship for descent.

"Matthias is infected with one of those parasites. I was hoping London would be able to help, but... at this point I think we may need your wife. Would it be possible to ask you to wait until I find them? Keep an ear on the channels to see if all hell broke loose on *The*

Olympia, if the situation was handled and it's safe to go back, or if we need to haul ass and go find your wife? Both of them will need medical assistance. I'm just not sure how to best approach it."

"I had no intention of leaving until Doctor Davies was on board this ship, sir. I'm going to drop us to a low power state. I didn't get the chance to refuel so I want to make sure we're good for the flight, but we'll still have radio contact. Make sure you sync up the helmets to the drop ship's channel so we can communicate and let me know when you're on your way back. We'll be landing near the defunct outpost dock shortly. It's a mess in there, so stay safe."

The vessel dipped beneath them as Hunter guided it to the main entrance on far end of the outpost. The domed structure was pitch black and ominous. It stretched far across the rocky terrain. Hitomi began syncing up the helmets in an attempt to focus on anything other than the death of her partner and the unknowns that laid before her.

Temple took a knee and set his gloved hand on Matthias' head. The young man stirred after a moment of resistance. He looked up at the captain with confusion and obvious exhaustion. His body was hitting its limit. He was tired of fighting the infection, tired of fighting a losing battle. His stomach felt as if it had been torn to ribbons.

"We're about to dock. We're going to get you help as soon as we retrieve London," Temple promised.

"I'll get suited up," Matthias grumbled.

"No need. You stay here with Hunter. You don't need to add any further stresses to your body, especially when we don't know what we're dealing with. I simply wanted to let you know we've arrived so you don't worry and remind you to take your insulin. Go back to sleep," Temple commanded.

Matthias looked at him warily but relented with a soft nod. He didn't feel like arguing or adding extra stress to his wounded innards.

Temple softly brushed his hair back out of his face and smiled.

"I'm proud of you, I need you to know that. You're a nova, and I'm proud of how far you've come, how brightly you shine," he said quietly before he stood. He looked at his phone. "We'll be there soon, London. Hang on."

"Don't leave..." they cried.

"I won't. I'm handing the phone to Hunter. We won't leave you."

He took the powered helmet from Hitomi and secured it over his head, letting the artificial oxygen hit his lungs like a gust of wind. Then, he carefully handed his device over with an immense amount of care, as if it were a precious thing, one he would die without. Hunter took it and set it upright on the ship's console so he could monitor the office.

"Touchdown in thirty seconds; prepping the bay for dock attachment. Give me a second before you disembark so I can get an oxygen mask on Matthias so that nothing happens to him when you open the door. Godspeed, Captain," Hunter said with a firm nod.

"Godspeed, Hunter," Temple replied with a soft inflection.

"Everything alright, sir?"

"My son's name was Hunter... You're a fine man, a good man. I'm sorry about your daughter."

"Go get that spitfire of a partner of yours, Captain Davies. I'll be here when you're ready. I'll call the missus and let her know we're coming and to prepare for several emergencies. They're going to be fine."

Temple and Hitomi, helmets secured, and minds steeled for departure, approached the loading door at the rear of the ship. The small vessel rumbled as the landing gear unfurled beneath them. They felt it make contact with the magnetic disc in the loading dock, securing it firmly to the surface with a powerful force. Hunter grabbed a face mask and secured it around his mouth as he engaged the interior gravity to keep them safe when the door opened. He knelt beside Matthias and began equipping him with the proper gear and a blanket to keep him comfortable during the upcoming wait.

"Are we good?" Temple inquired.

"Yes, sir. I'll keep him safe," Hunter promised.

As Temple prepared to disembark, the glimmer of something in the storage closet caught his eye. It was an emergency pistol, a sleek one with nary a fingerprint to be seen. Weaponry was not an abundant thing in the Project, but it was kept on board most ships as a precaution to handle troublesome individuals should the need arise. He pulled it from the rack and laid it in the crook of his amputated arm. Shakily, he loaded a full box of ammunition into it. The door chimed that it was safe to leave the ship, so he readied himself and stepped out into the darkness.

Hitomi followed close behind, sliding a few bullets into the chamber of a rifle she had snatched from the closet. The drop ship's door shut behind them and draped the small dock in shadow. The majority of the defunct outpost held little in the means of necessity when it came to matters of keeping humans alive. It wasted too much power, so they kept it in a low state for the irregular drops and an excess of storage for construction parts.

They pressed onward into the main holding area that was half finished and wide open. Open enough that it felt ominous and foreboding. The ceiling, made of beveled pieces of thick glass, opened to a view of the universe above them. A few stacks of large metal pieces, covered by a gently billowing tarp, sat in the center of the room. It was meant to be a check-in zone for patients and injured crew that needed processing before being sent to rooms for treatment.

Temple could see the beginnings of an auditorium-style operating room at his side. The large, intense overhead light that hung above a welded table in the center was limp. The wires that strung it to the half-finished power grid in the ceiling were taut from the unnatural bend of the arm. It looked like a strung-up body dangling from the rafters.

A grand foyer above overlooked the waiting area, though he was unsure of what the rooms hidden in the darkness just beyond the railings were for. The elevator shaft was open and powerless, but footprints could be seen inside from the small specks of dust workers once trailed in from their ships.

"This place could have been beautiful," Hitomi noted.

"So much of this fucking project could have been," Temple reminded. "Did you know?"

"Know what?"

"When you proposed the question to me the other day, about our galaxy back home being terraformed in our absence. Did you ask that question because you knew?"

"I had a hunch. Something Liza said during one of our late-night conversations got my mind running down that path, and it was hard to step off it."

"I feel like such an—"

Hitomi set her palm on Temple's chest. He stopped and turned his eyes to follow her outstretched hand, noticing the bit of movement in the shadows that caught her attention. A form walked by a semi-translucent tarp that hung over the back half of the lobby. His brows furrowed; his grip tightened on the pistol.

"Can we fathom to guess that the bodies that were delivered got back up?" Hitomi proposed.

"I would say that's a reasonable hypothesis, yes," Temple mused.

"Those nightmares in *The Olympia* morgue were probably infected with that... whatever Liza mentioned, which means we're dealing with... fucking hell... I can't believe I'm saying this... Are we dealing with zombies?"

"I would say so, in a sense. It's definitely not natural. It's hard to know whether or not they're still *themselves* in there, though. From the bit of data Matthias was able to pull, it sounds like a parasite that takes over the brains of its hosts, so they may be aware of the situation, only numbed to it with the infection. I can honestly believe that London was conversing with that last corpse, that it may still have been sentient in a sense. But that's just a theory. I'm a geologist for a reason, rocks make sense. People don't. Honestly? I didn't get enough of a look to really contemplate it. I don't think I want to, either. It'll make it harder to pull the trigger."

"Be careful, then. You were a horrible shot even when you had both of your hands."

Temple scoffed, and a large smile crept over his face. He held his pistol firmly, kept his finger at the ready, and pressed forward.

It took little time for them to realize that something was amiss as they approached the shadowy half of the outpost. As Hitomi pulled back the tarp, she found the next chamber overflowing with aggressive, shifting plant life. They warbled and twisted in the darkness, lining the walls and bursting through the unfinished pipework above. It was muggy, the moisture of the ecosystem in bloom caused humidity to cling to the tarp. She had to wipe the condensation from her visor to get a proper look at the area.

"Did London expand the garden?" Hitomi asked, half-jokingly.

Temple hit the comm switch on the side of his helmet, "Hunter, you said nothing was amiss when you arrived, correct? In the hospital outpost?"

"Correct. It was cold, empty, and pretty barren," Hunter confirmed.

"No plants?"

A moment of silence broke up the conversation.

"No, just metal and tarps," he added.

"Thank you," Temple said as he cut off the feed.

"So, all of this grew in the... what, few hours since the drop was made?" Hitomi asked in utter disbelief.

"I think they woke something up with their meddling on Elysium. Something old and angry," Temple replied as he stepped onto the mossy, wet ground. His foot sunk in the soft, curled green bundles and the squelch that echoed up into the ward was noticeable.

"You can't be serious."

"Sadly, I am. We're not dealing with something our understanding of science can explain. We were away from Earth for long enough that things could have, and probably did, drastically change. Right now, it doesn't need an explanation. Right now, we need to save London. I don't need to know the why."

Hitomi looked up at a thick, twisted braid of leaves and traced its trail into a pipe above. She scanned the room for the unknown entity that wandered through the darkness, rifle aimed before her with rigid precision. Temple followed close behind, checking the empty offices for movement as they made their way deeper into the outpost.

The figure seemed to have vanished, lost in the shadows of the outpost. Temple was afraid it had retreated down through the corridor they needed to follow into the research center that stood between his home and his current position. It would be easy for it to get the jump on them in the mess of rooms and materials.

They treaded carefully into the moist corridor, studying the walls of crawling greenery as they went. Large mushrooms drooped under the heavy weight of their caps, and the small, fluffy yellow puffs Temple noticed in the camera view of London's office floated softly through the air. The pollen clung to their suits, turning the black garments golden with the unnatural hue of their unstable forms.

"I wonder," Temple pondered as he looked at an open control box on the wall, "if the issues with the doors arose from this infection, for lack of a better term. Maybe something was crawling through the circuitry, and we simply never knew."

"Do you think this has been going on that long?" Hitomi asked.

"Possibly. We can assume these mutations have been going on for a while. It's not hard to imagine that one of the bodies they had at some point may have stirred up something, that a bit of something fell off of a cadaver and ended up in the walls of the outpost during a detox. Hell, it's probably the moldy bastard in the morgue. Maybe Liza was onto something. Maybe this issue was a long-standing problem that somehow became heightened when Zeus started meddling. Elysium wasn't the first colony to fall," he reminded.

Hitomi cupped a large purple bloom in her gloved hand. It was nearly the size of her head. She could see its roots had spread across a window in the corridor wall. The faint shimmer of starlight could be seen through the cross-stitched pattern of its crawling life support. If the situation weren't so dire, she'd be fascinated by it. It made her realize how much she missed Earth. Despite its flaws and wear, the lush and bountiful environments were a calming thing she desperately needed to return to.

Her thoughts were interrupted by Temple softly tapping her shoulder. She slowly turned her eyes to the side and steadied her rifle. Masked by shadows, jerking and croaking, stood a corpse half-hidden by a corner that turned into the research wing. The body would occasionally shift back into view before it pulled away. The arm seemed stretched to an unnatural length.

Temple and Hitomi crept forward, keeping to the shadows as best they could. Neither of them was trained for this, neither had enough intel to properly gauge how to approach this, whether or not these monstrosities could see, whether or not a bullet could stop them.

The corpse's arm was torn free of its socket, held together by a stitching of roots like a child's toy dangling by threads. The neck was shredded, and the skull hung so far back that it bounced against its shoulder blades as it moved. The jittery manner in which it shifted looked like a computer glitch, a ghost phasing in and out of existence.

Hitomi emptied her lungs and fired, sniping straight through the skull. A second shot flew through the exposed cervical spine. The impact caused the head to completely detach and topple to the ground, sending brain matter and green sludge spraying across the floor. Its broken mouth continued to snap and bite at nothing. Empty eye sockets left it blind to the environment. The headless body continued to walk, wandering by the duo back toward the ward.

As it turned into corridor, a wriggling black tube broke through the viscera of its neck. The sinew-and-gore-covered mouth gnashed at the air, sending a fountain of sludge out of its throat that coated the body it piloted unsteadily. Hitomi lifted her rifle again, but Temple set his hand on the barrel and pushed it down.

"Don't waste the ammo," he said quietly.

Hitomi nodded and waited until the body was safely out of view before she moved. Once it wandered into an office, she hurriedly closed the door in the hopes of keeping it locked inside, lessening the chance of having to deal with it on their return. So long as it held minimal power, the door would keep it trapped.

They pressed onward into the research outpost. It was overrun by heavy hanging leaves and dripping condensation from the new life springing forth from the metal. Temple felt as if he had been dropped into one of London's terrariums, a tiny world thriving without reasonable cause, thriving because it could.

The research outpost was nearly three-fourths complete in its construction before the project was halted. The tiny lab pods lining the walls held crates of equipment that hopeful researchers once planned to use to better humanity's survival. Temple saw another corpse in one of the rooms. It rammed its head over and over into a window. Green-tinged blood ran down its broken skull, down the clear pane.

A writhing worm-like creature wriggled out of a gaping hole in its head, snapping at the air with rings of teeth covered in blood and viscera like a snake disturbed in its nest. It looked similar to the monstrosity that took Temple's arm from him. The exit to the room it was in seemed to have been barricaded after entry. A large metal plate rested against the door; the glint of it was visible through the gore-coated pane of glass. Temple ascertained that it must have knocked it over with its frantic, mindless movements, trapping itself by accident.

With slow steps, the captain continued moving. His eyes never left the window until he was sure the corpse had not spotted them. They pushed through the thick overgrowth that seemed to be rising taller with each passing second. He turned the comm channel back on and radioed Hunter.

"We're about through the research outpost. Any word from London?" he asked.

"No. I've made sure to let them know I'm still here, but they're quiet," Hunter explained.

"Thank you. Make sure you keep the ship door shut. These freaks don't go down easily, and we don't need you two hurt."

"Good to know. Stay safe but hurry. It sounds like *The Olympia* has fallen. Communication has been fully severed. We may not have a lot of time to pull this off."

Hunter disconnected the call and exhaled. The flurry of incoming messages and updates that overwhelmed his console felt rapturous. It would seem the populace was angry enough to collapse the Project, and Hunter wasn't sure what would remain in the razed remnants after the fighting ceased. Somehow, he had to believe that the regular souls in this mess would overpower those in charge, that they would survive if they played their cards right.

A clashing chorus of cries to burn Zeus to the ground and Zeus' own calls of calm and false concern waged war on the radio waves.

Don't believe the lies!

Doctor Fontaine has misled you.

Overtake The Olympia!

Burn the bodies!

I don't know who to trust!

Kill anyone involved with Elysium, we aren't safe!

WE'RE DOOMED

It was an overload of information that suddenly died, as if the communications hub on *The Olympia* either pulled the plug to cease the mania, or the ship simply collapsed under the weight of the corpses and chaos. It grew too quiet too quickly. He rubbed his eyes and looked at the phone screen. He saw movement in the hallway behind London. A shadow crept across the low-lit wall. He watched for a moment, trying to ascertain what the disturbance was.

As he went to call Temple to warn him, his finger stopped just before it touched the button. The sharp, pained gasping noise that echoed in the small ship caused him to pause.

"Matthias? Everything okay?" Hunter asked as he turned to look behind him.

Matthias grasped his throat and stomach. He curled up on the floor and wheezed. Hunter spun the chair around and approached. He set his hand on the young man's back. The heat that radiated off of his spine was akin to scalding embers. He could feel something writhing in the young admin's body, pressing against his flesh with such force it rippled like the surface of a disturbed lake.

He folded in on himself, gagging as something forced itself up his throat. His neck bulged and his eyes, watering and wide with fear, grabbed onto Hunter for help, for something to hold onto. Hunter took his hand and watched with concern as he seemed to accept this damning fate. As if the young man knew what awaited him, knew it would be worthless to fight.

With a loud, retching motion, Matthias coughed up a squirming bundle of black tendrils. They forced themselves between his lips, throttling his ability to breath and speak, filling his mouth with enough mass that he could feel his teeth shift in his gums. They whipped angrily, like an octopus shoved into his maw, and they moved with such force his jaw dislocated on the right.

Tears of agony rolled down his cheeks as more broke through his nose, and trails of blood ran down his nostrils and dripped onto the floor. Hunter grabbed hold of one of the writhing anomalies and attempted to pull, attempted to free it from Matthias' body, but the contact with it burned like acid, and the slick surface of it made it impossible to handle. Still, he persisted, wrenching the parasite with as much strength as he could with a desperation to save the young man from a horrible demise.

Matthias wanted to scream. He retched and gagged, but the parasite had incubated much too long. It was massive. It felt as if his insides were being pulled out through his mouth. The tendrils wrapped themselves around Hunter's arms. He used it as leverage and planted his feet firmly on the ground as it wrapped him up like a spider trying to cocoon its prey.

With one harsh, final tug, Hunter ripped the beast from Matthias' body. The admin collapsed onto the ground, writhing in agony. Wheezing with drool and blood dripping from his mouth, he jerked and shuddered as the last of his neurons fired before his eyes rolled up into his head from the shock. The brief, freeing moment of relief from his innards being emptied left him euphoric in the split second before his body gave out on him.

The parasite fought to wrap itself around Hunter. The bulbous body that had settled inside of Matthias' stomach pumped like an overworked heart, throbbing and undulating with aggressive thumping. A long sick-covered tube ran from its rounded abdomen into Matthias' mouth, coiling along the floor for a moment before pulling taut as it lunged at the pilot. The umbilical cord remained connected to the admin's innards. As the infection moved, it yanked his frame across the floor.

The heft of the alien shot down atop Hunter. The tendrils wrapped around his throat like a snake. The combined force of its mass and vicious movements knocked him to the ground before he could steady himself. It clamored to strangle him, to choke the life from his lungs.

Hunter's head bounced off the metal flooring hard enough to send shockwaves of pain through his neck and stun his body, enough to lose his grip. As he gasped, one of the tendrils shot down into his mouth, piercing him through the back of the skull and severing his spinal cord. He stopped resisting, stopped fighting, and fell dead in a single breath's time.

A light on the dash began blinking, and the unanswered call rang out into the drop ship as the parasite frantically tried to break free of the metal casing it found itself trapped in. The name on the screen read '*Doctor McCall – Shangri-La Team*'.

XVIII

The door to the morgue entrance sat slightly ajar. A few large round leaves broke through the small opening. The decontamination chamber was slick with condensation, and the control panel hung loose on the wall as the heft of newly grown plant life broke through the hardwiring of the outpost. Temple set his pistol down and slid his fingers into the crack of the door, pulling with as much strength as he could muster to try and pry it open. Hitomi assisted, planting her feet as firmly as she could against the slick floor to gain some leverage.

The door resisted their attempts for a brief moment until the force of the overgrown greenery on the other side had enough momentum to push through like a flood. The door slid open, and a wall of thick ivy tumbled into the chamber.

It came crashing down, sending another corpse tumbling though the opening, wailing with pained, shrill sounds. A massive, parasitic growth on its head squirmed and pulsated like a tumor. Its left eye was enlarged, attached to the mass and moving wildly as it try to hone in on a target. The ribcage was exposed, internal organs hung down over their midsection, and the lab coat over their frame was stained green and yellow.

Hitomi snatched up her rifle and took aim, sending a well-placed shot through the growth. It burst like a pustule. A fetid, sickly liquid sprayed out across the landscape. The roots and plants below began to sizzle from the contact of it, and a swarm of worm-like creatures scrambled for darkness as the safety of the skin sack was broken. The corpse stumbled, so Hitomi unloaded another shot. Temple picked up his pistol and aimed for its legs to stop it from moving too close.

It toppled to the ground from the excess of damage, its frame too weak to sustain itself from the rot and mold that overtook it. The worms swam back into the corpse, trying to avoid the lights that singed their nocturnal flesh as a flood of brain matter spilled out onto the ground.

"We need to burn it," Temple noted as he tried to compose himself. "Help me carry it."

Hitomi grabbed its legs and pulled it into the morgue, dragging its decayed flesh across the plants with enough force that its abdomen tore completely and smeared its organs across the bundles of woven vines and roots.

Temple stepped into the morgue and raced to the cremation oven. He powered it on and urged Hitomi to follow. Though the body tried to struggle, it was unable to fight back at a quick enough pace to be a threat. The wayward worms were unable to control the limbs properly, unable to pilot the husk as they fought to find darkness when the ripped flesh disturbed their nest. Hitomi and Temple quickly lifted the sagging corpse and tossed it into the building heat, then locked the oven door with a resounding clang.

The old friends took a moment to catch their breath. The only thing that stood between them and London was the staircase, but they needed to steel themselves for the trek back with a wounded body in tow.

"What the fuck is that?" Hitomi asked, pointing to the gurney near the bay door.

"A project of Liza's..." Temple trailed off, looking at the nightmarish scene before him.

The case was broken, and a trail of thick, coagulated mold ran down the side of the metal table. Bulbous tubes that initially appeared to be wires crawled down onto the floor, breaking through the embalming drain and busted plastic. As Temple approached, he could see they were roots attempting to burrow into the cold metal. The mouth of the half-body inside the damp case snapped at them, and its broken fingers pounded into the case with desperation as it tried to escape.

The yellow pollen that flew around the room escaped from the craters and sunken pores across its decayed flesh. The roots that broke free of its frame scrambled into nearby technology, causing several of the morgue trays to open and close rapidly. The lights continued to flicker, the rhythm matching the thump of the vines like arteries. This creature was rooted into the outpost, controlling it.

"Mur...der," it croaked.

Temple recognized it. Recognized the familiar tone that crept up through the stairwell and called him down to this damned place when he last arrived home. This demon. This fucking demon ruined everything. The malfunctioning doors, the whispering sounds, the chaos wrought in his home came from this creature, and the anger boiling over within him became too much.

It shot its hand out through the crack. Its bent and shattered fingers tried to grab hold of his spacesuit. Temple lifted his pistol and aimed at its head, but Hitomi grabbed his wrist to stop him.

"Let go!" Temple demanded.

"Calm down. We don't know what it will do to the outpost if we kill it. We need to secure London first. You kill the brain..."

"The body goes with it. Fuck..." Temple lowered his gun.

He cursed the world around him, cursed the corpse and the hell it brought with it. Hitomi was right. This was no longer merely an outpost. It was a living, breathing thing that held some sense of sentience and was desperately fighting against them as if they were an infection that came to destroy the system from within. It breathed, it blinked, and it knew something treaded along its innards with enough knowledge to fight back. Severing that brain stem would severe the functionality, and he needed to prioritize London over his rage.

Hitomi looked around the morgue, noticing the opened body trays that lined the lower levels of the shelves. Many of them were dented, covered in blood and broken bits of fingernails as the re-animated occupants forced themselves free of the cold bindings. A few strands of flesh hung off of the trays. She was concerned about moving forward, about finding her lover among the wreckage. Still, she knew she needed to continue to reach that staircase.

"Hunter, we're at the morgue," Temple called into the comm channel.

He was met with silence.

"Hunter? Matthias?"

The call refused to connect.

"That's bad," Hitomi noted.

"We need to hurry," Temple urged.

He pushed by her and walked around the middle column of body trays. The morgue floor was slick from the mixture of condensation and bodily fluids. He could feel the heavy boots of his spacesuit struggle to plant firmly to the ground as he pushed onward. His eyes locked onto a familiar form, and though he tried to stop her, Hitomi's heartbreak proved too powerful for his exhausted hand to intervene.

Liza laid on a tray that struggled to open as the system malfunctioned, face half covered by a body bag and eyes sunken into her skull. Her lab coat was painted copper with dried, cold blood, and her skin was an unhealthy grey. Glasses shattered and head dented, she remained motionless.

Temple didn't know which outcome was worse. No, he did not want to see Liza writhing and infected, but he could never have fathomed how hard it would be to look down upon the dead body and listen to his dear friend weep in anguish over her corpse.

"What are we doing here, Temple?" Hitomi asked again, desperate for answers, for some sort of clarity and reason for this madness.

He didn't have anything to offer. Nothing he could say would soothe the ache. The universe was eating them alive, one by one, like grapes plucked from a vine until it was barren and fruitless. Humanity was crumbling. It would no longer exist after this day. Try as he might, hard as he would fight against it, this would end in disaster. Whether from the wrath of a vengeful Earth fighting back against the sickness of humanity's return, or of a man-made virus that shredded its hosts alive from the inside out, it didn't matter. Their species would not survive to see the morning. All he could do was go find London and wait out the end. That was all he needed to do. Everything else was fleeting.

Some horrors were not worth understanding. He accepted that, and he knew that fighting against those unknowns would only do more harm. Some wars were not meant to be fought; some were merely meant to be watched. And he would, with London by his side, and he would be satisfied knowing it was enough.

No hypothesis or theory, no amount of data or research, would ever justify, clarify, or rectify this genocide. And it needn't be rectified. It simply needed to be. He simply needed to let it go and accept it.

"I'm going to get my lover," Temple stated.

"And if they're the same as mine?" Hitomi proposed.

"Hitomi—"

"I'll be up in a bit... Let me... wrap my mind around this. Let me say goodbye."

Temple gripped her shoulder tight. It would be impossible for him to formulate any worthwhile response or comforting phrase to soothe this ache. He needed to let her process. He knew he needed to prepare himself for a similar experience. So, he let her be and continued toward the far end of the morgue.

The stairwell door was open. A bloody handprint was pressed over the control panel. He began his ascent through the dark tunnel with quiet, slow motions. The air was heavy with the glowing yellow pollen, lighting up the shadows like fireflies in the heat of summer. The staircase creaked, so he ensured his motions were precise and controlled to lower the chance of startling whatever may be lingering above him. The weight of his injury and the pharmaceuticals, amplified with the anxiety of the radio silence from the drop ship and the unknown of what awaited him above, left him lightheaded.

The lab was pitch black, and he refused to check it for movement, refused to waste one more second delaying what was to come. Something moved in that blackness, but he didn't acknowledge it.

Setting foot on the landing of the main floor, he saw the small window in the door was broken, its remnants littered the ground. Shredded bits of thick vines and what appeared to be flesh were tangled in the jagged edges of the shattered pane. The soft crunch beneath his boot echoed as he pushed through the opening just enough to slip inside. The corridor light flickered above him. The plants in the hydroponics stations overflowed onto the floor, creating a cascading waterfall that tangled and sprawled. The leaves and blooms glistened with yellow pollen. His visor fogged from the humidity.

He stepped into the next room and sighed heavily. London was on their side with their arm curled above their head, draped in the soft glow of the dimming grow lights. Silas, broken free of its container down below in the chaos, sat atop London's shoulder. The arachnid seemed agitated. It hissed at his approach, and its legs went rigid as it prepared itself to attack.

Temple set his pistol down and lifted his hand to show he meant no harm, "Silas, it's me."

"Temple?"

"Hi, love. I'm here. I'm right behind you."

London shakily lifted their hand and set their finger atop Silas' round body. It reacted to their touch and skittered up onto their hand as they placed it atop their shoulder, unable to muster enough strength to lower their limb to the ground again. Temple slowly went to their side and set his palm atop their head.

"Are you breathing alright?" Temple asked.

"I don't know," they replied quietly.

Temple carefully slid his hand under their body and lifted them from the cold metal flooring. They were stiff from being so motionless for so long. Temple struggled to hold them with his missing arm, but he was as careful as he could be so as to not injure them further. As their head rolled to the side, he felt his blood run cold.

The long, slender spike that punctured their throat was lost among a layer of coral pink and silver mushrooms that refused to pull away from where they had rooted to the floor for a moment. Their right eye was milky, reflecting a vast array of soft, warm hues like a pearl under a spotlight. And, as he held them, he realized they were not breathing. Their sweatpants were soaked in blood. Only their left eye blinked. Their skin was paler than normal, and it was apparent they were not entirely alive. Not as dead as the others, but still a corpse, nonetheless.

"Hi, beautiful," Temple said with a soft, tender tone.

He watched as Silas climbed up his suit, discovering new textures and sensations before it wandered off onto the console to explore further knowing its protector was safe.

"I'm sorry," London whispered.

"So am I. I'm never going to leave your side again. I swear it. Can you walk?"

"I don't know."

"We have a drop ship ready to go. Let me get Hitomi so she can..."

Do what? Where could they go? What would leaving accomplish?

"Don't leave," London begged.

"I won't."

Temple held them close to his chest to let them feel reassured, for them to reconnect, and for his own peace of mind to embrace the reality of the situation. He was home; he was holding them. That was all that mattered for the moment.

"I'd carry you myself if I could," Temple promised.

"Hold me..." they whispered.

He did. As tight as he could. His eyes drifted up to the console and the flood of chaotic, angered warnings that lined their computer. They came in slowly, unable to fully connect with the damage to the outpost, but the fall of Zeus was happening in real time before his eyes, captured in flashing notification boxes and urgent messages that would go unanswered.

He saw a familiar name pop up on the screen, with a scared and vulnerable message attached. It was Matthias. It was a soft apology. A note of fear, of pleading. He fixed London so they were leaning against him, so he was able to hold them with his damaged arm, and attempted to find the video call screen that was still connected to his phone in the drop ship among the influx of messages.

What he saw once the window was pulled up signified the end of it all. Slumped in the pilot's chair, Matthias sat with heavy, reddened eyes. Blood trickled down his face from both nostrils and a fleshy tube hung out of his mouth. It draped over his shoulder, over the headrest of the seat, and dangled in the air. The other end connected to a massive creature that undulated on the ceiling of the ship. It pumped with each heavy beat of his heart, constricted with each pained inhale he tried to take.

Matthias shakily lifted his phone and sent another message.

'I'm scared.'

"I'm right here," Temple assured.

Matthias' bloodshot eyes struggled to focus. But he saw London, saw the fungal growth sprawling across their face, and how they did not acknowledge him. It resigned him to his fate, but he felt calmer knowing Temple had finally found them, that he was able to hold them in his arms. That he himself was able to see his beloved mentor and friend one last time.

The cord that kept the parasite connected to the half-dead Matthias constricted like an artery, feeding the beast with his own life force. He did not want to die connected to it. He did not want to be the reason it still lived.

Matthias shakily lifted up his pocketknife.

'Stay with me, please', he typed slowly with weakened fingers. He could feel the strain on his body, the dehydration from the lack of insulin and the draining of his energy. Damn the unholy creature that made him its host. Damn it to hell.

"I will," Temple promised. "And I *will* come get you. We'll walk through this ending together, whatever happens. I swear it to you, by the time you next open your eyes, in whatever manner you do, I will be there beside you. This is home. You're home, and you're safe and here to stay. Remember that and wait for me. Don't be scared. I'm so proud of you, so is London..."

Matthias nodded, comforted by the fact that he would be beside

them soon, in whatever manner this insanity would bring them together again. In death, he would finally be beside his family in the
manner he was meant to be.

He bit down on the tube, and the creature shuddered and bounced
on the ceiling. He grabbed onto the slick, fleshy substance and hacked
away at it with the knife. Cleaving through it, a spray of blood shot out
onto the console. The arachnid-like monstrosity hissed like a leaking
gas tank, its tendrils curled in shock from the sudden severing of
its food source. Matthias dropped the knife and collapsed into the
console. His back only rose a handful of times before he was finally
granted the peace of the long sleep he was so desperate to find.

Temple spoke to him firmly, loud enough that he could hear, loud
enough for him to know he had not left and would not leave until
that last breath was taken and, most importantly, that he would come
back for him when the time was right. His own breaking heart and
quaking voice refused to relent until that death rattled echoed out into
the office.

When the parasite finally lost its grip on the ceiling and fell to the
floor, Temple disconnected the call and held onto London as tight as
his weakened grip would allow. They did not seem to register any of
what had happened. He was thankful; they didn't need to see it, didn't
need to know the fate of their sweet student they longed so desperately
to see.

For once in his life, Temple Davies did not know what to do. No
plan could be made. No escape route could be thought of. Their ship
was down, their pilot was dead, and it would seem that every safe haven
in the universe had fallen. He set his hand against their neck. No pulse
could be found. His palm was placed upon their chest. Their lungs did
not move.

Shakily, he undid their respirator and let it fall to the ground. Their lips were stained with blood. Temple softly stroked their cheek with his thumb. He noticed their left eye, though still blue and vast as an ocean, did not focus. It looked like a watercolor mess on a napkin, split and spilling over the white.

"Can you... see?" Temple asked.

"I don't know."

"Give me a few minutes, okay? I need to make sure we're safe."

"Hurry."

London lifted their hand and held up a tangled necklace. It was one Temple knew well. He took it from them and promised he would pass it along to its rightful owner, then return to them in the blink of an eye and never leave them again.

Temple gently laid them on the floor, on their back at a more comfortable angle. He grabbed a throw blanket and laid it over them, mostly for his own peace of mind. He needed to find Hitomi, needed to figure out what the hell he was doing. He was spiraling, overwhelmed and panicked and in need of a clear mind to help talk through this nightmare.

He raced back down the staircase but came to an abrupt stop when he heard something topple over in the lab. He peered around the corner and looked into the darkness. A silhouetted figure shuddered. Its head rolled back and forth, hitching as it moved to the left, as if the bones refused the movement. The skull was coated in yellow pollen, creating a glowing signal through the broken visor of the space helmet over its head. It shot through the shadows like a lighthouse.

Temple quietly crept by it once he was sure it wasn't looking and made his way down to the morgue. He skidded into the room.

"Hitomi, we need..."

The blood had already begun to coagulate. The two women, wrapped together in death, laid motionless. The rifle was clutched between them, and the remnants of an irreversible action were painted brightly in the form of a discarded helmet and sticky locks of hair. Temple knelt beside his friend and secured the locket around her neck.

In the unsteady lights, it looked as though she was smiling. It was enough.

He slowly sat down and let himself have a moment to breathe, to grieve, and wrap his mind around the heft of death around him. He took in the overflowing greenery, the bountiful blooms and peaceful serenity of it all. He hadn't realized how desperately he missed it. Missed the small yard he fenced in himself, one that held such lovely things, where so many memories were made. Missed the sensation of grass beneath his feet. The way his lover's hair shimmered in real sunlight. The joy of feeling alive.

This was as close as he'd get to that pleasure, that comfort again in this lifetime. London's words traipsed through his mind, and he felt himself smile.

I suppose my grave should be littered with flowers.

How beautiful this mausoleum was.

How beautiful his London was.

He pushed himself up and decided to accept the reality of the situation. He ensured the oven timer was set to shut off in a few hours and turned the lights off so as not waste any more precious power. As much as he wanted to kill the fungal mess by the bay door, he decided to let it live. Let it pump life into this strange new ecosystem it built out of nothingness and allow it to cover their home in the safety of soil and stems.

The glow of the oven window flickered like a fireplace, casting red and orange lights over the darkened room. He closed the morgue stairwell door as best he could, then made his way back to his lover.

The last remaining corpse still stood in the lab, knocking things left and right with a guttural noise. It sounded like the voices he had heard weeks ago during his leave. The sounds that tormented his lover. The residual hauntings of the bodies filtered through the halls, screaming for vengeance and peace. This hive-mind was angry, and he felt they were justified in their rage and sorrow. This old, weary power was in need of a long sleep without humanity interfering. The angered voices of a millennia of agony, lost in the metal halls of a tiny outpost on a forgotten moon, sounded so scared. He pitied it. Pitied the things that humanity had done to cause this chaos.

It whipped its head around upon hearing his approach.

"Pain..."

"There will be *no more pain*," Temple promised.

"It... hurts..."

"There will be no more pain."

"The roots... the earth... my body... tainted by *you*."

"We won't hurt you any longer. I swear it. Rest now."

"Rest..."

"A well-deserved one. For us all."

The corpse straightened up and turned to face him. The neck cracked as it tilted its heavy, root-covered skull to face him. He did not lift his pistol. He did not pose a threat. It knew. This creature, whatever it was at its core, seemed to understand this. He could theorize until the stars burned out, pose many possibilities, and hypothesize until he grew old and grey, and never find a conclusive answer to any of this. He wasn't sure he needed to, either.

"Earth will not suffer at the hands of humanity any longer. And you can stay. You are welcome here," Temple assured.

It moved forward, lifting its broken, twisted arm upward with strained motions. The limb was shredded, and bone was visible beneath the flaps of the spacesuit. He could see its eyes from this distance, and he felt the need to turn away out of fear and respect. It did not feel appropriate to gaze upon it. It felt old, ancient, and worthy of his respect.

It plucked a sharp, thin thorn from its face and handed it to him.

"Prove... it..."

Temple set his pistol down and pulled his helmet from his head. He looked at the familiar, sturdy piece of wood and plunged it deep into his neck. He felt his tendons tense, and a rush of something hit his system. It was intoxicating. It caused a fluttering in his lungs.

With a sharp, guttural release, the corpse collapsed into a heap on the ground, satisfied that this human would keep his word, satisfied in the knowledge that the plague that was humankind was eradicated from the galaxy. The helmet came loose and spun on the floor until it finally stopped at Temple's feet. Eyes, sunk deep into their sockets, flickered out with an array of colors before dimming. Draping the lab in darkness one final time.

Yes, humanity would no longer taint the universe with its touch, and what a freeing feeling it was to witness the calamity of it all. He felt lighter, enough that he was confident in leaving his pistol on the nearby medical tray. Helmet tucked under his arm, he continued his ascent with blurring eyes and a featherweight frame.

As Temple reached the top of the staircase, he grabbed hold of the broken window and closed the door behind him. The sharp, jagged pieces of glass tore through his spacesuit, piercing his rough palms enough to draw blood.

In the low light, he caught a glimpse of the frame of his lover in the doorway of their bedroom. He approached with cautious steps. He could see the strands of fungi stretching down across their body, see pale cream and mulberry blooms unfurl across their tangled hair. Even in death, they were divine. Even in death, he longed to hold them. Silas burrowed itself into the curves of the oyster mushrooms and savored the sensation of true life against its body.

"He's beautiful," London said happily.

"Who?" Temple questioned.

"Our boy... Can't you see him, Temple? Playing in the fields?"

Temple swallowed hard and took a shuddering breath.

"Oh... Temple?"

"Yes, love?"

"I think I'm dead."

Temple stood behind them and gazed into the warm, inviting space. His orchid bloomed the most vibrant hues of mulberry, purple, and burgundy he had ever laid eyes on. The dangerous yellow pollen that fell from its petals like rainfall no longer posed a threat. The houseplants draped over the bookshelf, tangled in the threads of their clothes, and made their bed with welcoming blooms. The small window dripped with condensation. It felt muggy and warm. In all his years of exploration, of research and travel, of sights both known and unknown that he was lucky to have seen, none of it compared to this.

It was a gift. A terrarium for them to spend eternity in.

"Are you going to leave me here?" London asked.

Their inquiry was answered by the sound of his helmet hitting the metal flooring. Finally, he kissed their cheek and buried his face in the curve of their shoulder. Desperate for connection, for the sensation of their flesh, he held them. His hand found their stomach, their trembling fingers wrapped around his, and for a beautiful moment, he swore he felt life inside of them. Whether or not it was true, he felt them, and it was enough.

He inhaled the familiar, comforting scents of earth and flora that wafted off their body. It was intoxicating, enough to dull the sensation of throttled oxygen in his lungs as the slow pull of death tugged on him. Death's hands were tender, and he felt welcomed in the release. If he were to become but a tree, rooted to this place with his budding orchid in his grasp, he would gladly accept it.

"Where else am I to go, London? Not a single place in the whole of this galaxy would ever be as lovely, as wonderful, as this. If this outpost is to be your home, it will also be mine. If it will be your grave, then it will also be mine. If you'll let me stay, I will tangle myself to you and never leave your side."

"I love you, Temple."

"I'm home. I'm finally... home."

London laid their head back against his shoulder and let him wrap them up in his embrace. His skin felt rigid. He could sense it tightening as if it were bark sprawling across a mighty oak. His body was giving out on him. His lungs were slowing; his brain was shutting down. It was time.

Suddenly, he felt light and was awash with realization at just how wounded his frame had been. How ravaged he had been by the unseen wear of a vicious cancer that left him weary and fatigued without his knowledge. He hadn't realized how ill he'd felt until he felt nothing at all, and oh, how freeing it was to be rid of the weight of humanity. To shirk off the layers of life and accept an eternity returned to the Earth he never believed he'd see again. Yes, it was time.

So, he lifted his lover into his arms, eliciting a playful laugh from London that was dreamy and childlike, and carried them to the bed. Tenderly, he laid them on the mattress, and using the last of his strength, he stripped out of his spacesuit and collapsed beside them atop the quilt of vines and blossoms. His damaged, wounded arm was hardening. The flesh left from the crumpled, hasty amputation was turning into the wooden rings of a tree, slowly reshaping before his eyes into a fully formed limb that would return what was lost to him in due time.

"A beautiful... grave... for us both..." Temple whispered as blood trickled down his chin. He coughed out harshly.

London lifted their weakened hand and wiped the tears away from his earthen-hued eyes. How deep and vast they were. How dearly they loved this man. No, they could no longer see him, but they could see the untold wonders of the universe in bloom around him as their vision—now freed of the confines of its human makeup—was able to focus on what lay beyond their mortal understanding. No, they could no longer see him, but they could sense him. And he was radiant.

A short, harsh death rattle escaped his lips, and the room was draped in silence.

London, eager to experience a forever among the sprawling world they were robbed of for so long, rested easy and waited for him to wake again. No longer stunted by their wounds, no longer needing to breathe, they felt alive. Finally, they felt alive. And their husband could no longer leave them. Where else in the universe could he go? Now that it all burned from humanity's hubris? The universe would never entice him again.

What a beautiful thing it was. The silence. The stars. The simplicity of this place.

Such a beautiful thing, and London felt comfortable closing their eyes knowing that Temple would still be there in the morning. They would root their new frames to the growth, to each other, and give themselves over to this tiny new Earth, sewn together with threads of ivy and the lifeblood of an old, forgotten power. Two corpses stitched up with vines and powdered with poppies to walk along corridors of metal and magnolia for the rest of time.

They would be the catalysts of a lush new world, isolated to a forgotten moon that was rapidly forming like a big bang in an empty pocket of space desperate for a fresh start with their dear Matthias by their side and a plethora of new experiences to discover at a slow pace that offered them hope and comforts. A new world, untouchable and wholly theirs. One they would protect. One they could control. One they would experience together in death and rebirth.

Tangled in roots and vines, the star-crossed lovers finally closed the vast space that cleaved apart their souls with relentless fervor. The stars could no longer come between them.

No, those old gods did not have any power here. Not anymore. Not when Mother Nature blessed this sanctum and forced them to lay down their swords. The war was finally over. And they too could now rest.

A Note from Timber Ghost Press

I f you enjoyed *The Scientist, the Spaceman, and the Stars Between Them*, please consider leaving a review on Amazon or Goodreads. Reviews help the authors and the press.

If you go to www.timberghostpress.com you can sign up for our newsletter so you can stay up-to-date on all our upcoming titles, plus you'll get informed of new horror flash fiction and poetry featured on our site monthly.

Take care and thanks for reading *The Scientist, the Spaceman, and the Stars Between Them!*

-Timber Ghost Press